MISTLETOE & MURDER

❄

SARAH HAMAKER

Copyright © 2021, Seshva Press. All rights reserved. Without limiting the rights under copyright reserved above, no part of this publication may be reproduced, stored in or introduced into a retrieval system, or transmitted, in any form, or by any means (electronic, mechanical, photocopying, recording, or otherwise) without the prior written permission of both the copyright owner and Seshva Press. Contact Sarah Hamaker via her website, sarahhamakerfiction.com.

This book is licensed for your personal enjoyment only. This book may not be resold or given away to other people. Thank you for respecting the hard work of this author.

✸ Created with Vellum

QUOTE

The truth, however ugly in itself, is always curious and beautiful to the seeker after it.

—*Agatha Christie, mystery writer*

CHAPTER 1

Thursday, December 20

Isabella Montoya entered the kitchen, the door swinging shut behind her. She plunked her empty tray on the counter with a clatter. "I think if some of the townsfolk weren't still around, those Thatchers would be popping the cork on a bottle of champagne in anticipation of the reading of the will."

"Don't let them get to you." Shelia Watts pulled a pan of hot grilled cheese and fruit chutney sandwiches from the oven and placed it on a hot pad.

"I'm trying not to, but you know Miss Heloise was more than my employer—she was like a godmother. I miss her." Isabella wouldn't give the relatives the satisfaction of seeing the hired help crying over the death of the family matriarch, Heloise Stratman Thatcher. Not that she saw any display of grief on the faces of the dozen or so family members who had dutifully trotted to Twin Oaks, Virginia, for the memorial service. If only they had shown Miss Heloise such care and consideration during her ninety-three years on earth.

"I think you were the only one who got along with Miss Heloise. Everyone else stayed away because of her sharp tongue." Shelia helped Isabella transfer the sandwiches to a clean serving tray.

Isabella handed her best friend a tray of crackers topped with salmon and a dollop of Greek yogurt. "She had her moments, but she was a grand old lady." She picked up the tray of sandwiches.

Isabella followed Shelia though the swinging door to the largest room in the mansion that dominated the end of what was commonly referred to as "founding fathers" lane. The Thatchers had been among the first to settle Twin Oaks back at the turn of the nineteenth century, and patriarch Aaron Thatcher had secured the choicest bit of land to build his sprawling Federalist house with its sweeping views of the Shenandoah Valley and distant Blue Ridge Mountains. Miss Heloise never tired of telling the story of how the Yankees burned that mansion to the ground—and destroyed the family's lumber yard—during the Civil War, leaving the Thatchers to eke out a living. Then, in the late 1880s, Miss Heloise's great-great-grandfather, Elias Thatcher, regained the family fortune by speculating on railroads. It was Elias who built the current house, a larger replica of the original.

Plastering on a smile, Isabella sailed into the parlor, tray held high as she maneuvered to the opposite side of the room from where Shelia offered hors d'oeuvres. Shelia was right about Miss Heloise rubbing people the wrong way. Miss Heloise did have a rather unfortunate way of pointing out the wrongness of a matter with all the finesse of a hammer. The fact that Miss Heloise was right didn't make her manner of delivery more palatable, as Isabella herself had found out when her employer had denounced Isabella's fiancé, Jay, as "a two-faced lout who will break your heart." Which Jay promptly did when he came back from a deployment to announce he'd married someone else.

Mentally shaking away thoughts of Jay's duplicity, Isabella lowered the tray halfway between her shoulder and waist to offer the sandwiches to Titus Simons, a paunchy man with a red florid face, and Lorna Hemes, a rail-thin woman whose tightly permed, shoulder-length hair framed her pointed face. "Would you like one?" She held out a stack of cocktail napkins with her other hand as the man reached for a sandwich.

"This place is worth a pretty penny, although who'd want it with all this Christmas greenery and decorations." Titus shoved the entire sandwich in his mouth.

Lorna took a napkin, then selected the smallest sandwich on the tray. "Good thing too, since we'll have to divide the proceeds from the sale of the house between twelve of us."

Isabella turned to serve other guests but was blocked by Janet Bothman, a middle-aged woman in a black stretch pantsuit that barely contained her generous curves.

Lorna nodded to the newcomer. "Janet, I haven't seen you since last summer."

Janet stepped around Isabella. "Oh, right, at the barbeque Titus threw on the Fourth of July."

Isabella started to sidle away, but Janet stopped her. "Hold on there. I want one of those sandwiches."

Of course you do. Turning back, Isabella held out the tray and onto her tongue.

Janet continued talking. "But you're off on the beneficiaries count, Lorna."

Lorna frowned. "What do you mean?"

Janet motioned for Isabella to stay put and snagged another hors d'oeuvre. "There are thirteen heirs."

Titus shook his head as Lorna started to speak, but Janet cut them both off. "You're forgetting about Alec Stratham."

"No one's forgetting about the long-lost cousin or nephew or whoever he is." Titus grabbed another sandwich from Isabella's tray.

Isabella should circulate among the room before these three ate all the sandwiches off her tray, but curiosity rooted her feet to the carpet at the mention of Alec's name. Miss Heloise had often spoken of her great-nephew, who was only a little older than Isabella's own twenty-seven years. Isabella had dusted his photo—prominently placed in the center of Miss Heloise's dresser—hundreds of times over the eight years she'd worked here, but had never met Alec in person. Shifting slightly back to station herself against the mantel, she fixed her gaze at the swatches of mistletoe and red ribbons around the top of the pocket doors that led to the dining room and waited to hear more.

"He likely won't even have heard about the death in time to make it here today. Anyway, his vote won't matter." Lorna waved her hand. "The other heirs agree with us on how to handle things."

Janet shushed her. "There's plenty of time to talk strategy once the will's been read."

Isabella took that as her cue to move to another location, holding out the tray to other relatives, and the pastor and his wife. All the while, the photographic image of Alec Stratham, his dark brown hair and dancing gray eyes, stayed with her.

❋

ALEC STRATHAM STARED UP AT THE MASSIVE BRICK MANSION IN THE gloomy light. A light snow had started to fall during his walk from the train station. He could have called an Uber, but after traveling since yesterday morning to get here, he wasn't about to climb into another mode of transportation. Hefting the duffle bag back on his shoulder, he headed for the front door. With any luck, all the non-relatives would have departed, leaving him to face the gauntlet of distant family members he had never met. If Great-Aunt Heloise hadn't sent him that last letter hinting of distress and subterfuge by an unnamed relative, he wouldn't be so troubled over her death.

Alec hesitated on the front porch. Should he ring the doorbell or walk in? Before he could decide, the door opened and an elderly couple emerged.

"Goodness gracious!" The woman put her hand to her chest and offered Alec a weak smile. "You startled me." She peered up at him as her companion shut the door behind him. "Do I know you?"

Alec summoned his own smile. "I don't think so, ma'am. It's been a long time since I visited Heloise."

"Why, you're Alec Stratham, am I right?" The man held out his hand. "You probably don't remember, but we met a few times the summer you stayed with your great-aunt when you were just a teenager. I'm the Reverend Paul Brown, and this is my wife, Margery."

Alec vaguely recalled a younger version of the minister coming by on a summer's evening to visit Heloise. "Kind of you to remember me."

"Not at all." Rev. Brown smiled at Alec. "Heloise talked often about you. She was very proud of your Army service."

"I can't believe she's gone." Alec straightened. "How was the memorial service? A couple of my flights were delayed, or I would have arrived in time."

"It was exactly as your aunt would have wished," Rev. Brown said.

"Not that those people cared." Margery's blue eyes sparked as her husband laid a hand on her shoulder. "You would have been one of the only true mourners among the relatives, that's for sure."

"Now, Margery, let's not stir the pot." Rev. Brown drew his wife's arm through his own. "We must be going. My door is always open, if you need a friendly ear." Rev. Brown handed Alec his card, then patted his shoulder before the minister ushered his wife toward the driveway.

Alec tucked the card into his pocket before entering the house. Closing the door, he put his things against the wall, then shed his coat and laid it on top of his duffle. The entryway hadn't changed a bit since he last saw it fifteen years ago as a gangly fourteen-year-old. Alec placed his hand on the top of the pineapple serving as the newel post on the carved banister that graced the sweeping staircase to the second floor. He could almost hear Heloise talking about how her great-great-grandfather Elias Thatcher had hired a carpenter all the way from England to carve it.

After savoring the moment of nostalgia, he headed toward the front parlor, where he could see a sliver of light from the half-open oak door. Taking a deep breath, he reached for the handle just as someone rang the doorbell. Might as well answer it and delay the awkward conversation with relatives he'd never met. Turning back to the entrance, Alec pulled open the heavy front door.

A man and a woman dressed in wool overcoats stood on the porch. The woman flashed her badge at him as she spoke, "I'm Detective Blanche Mullins, and this is Detective Jim Talbot. May we come in?"

Detective Mullins started forward as if to push Alec backwards into the house, but he held his ground. "What's this all about?"

The two detectives exchanged a glance. "Who are you?" Detective Talbot shot back.

Alec frowned at the classic diversionary tactic of responding to a question with a question. Two could play at that game. "If you've come to pay your respects, you're a little late." No need to tell them that he had missed the service too.

"We're not here to pay our respects," Detective Mullins said.

Alec leaned his shoulder against the door jamb as the snow continued to fall. Being trained as an Army sniper had conditioned him to ignore outside influences, such as hot or cold temperatures. "Then why are you here?"

"Can I help?" A male voice behind Alec inquired.

Alec turned. An older man in an impeccable pinstriped suit and silver rimmed glasses stood just behind the door.

The older man smiled at Alec. "You must be Alec Stratham. I'm Peter Wilson, Miss Heloise's estate attorney."

Alec nodded at the lawyer, then gestured toward the detectives. "They're detectives but won't tell me why they're here."

Wilson frowned. "What's this all about?"

"It's related to the death of Heloise Thatcher," Detective Talbot said.

"Then you'd better come in," Wilson responded.

With a shrug, Alec moved back to allow the pair to enter before closing the door firmly behind them. The attorney greeted them and exchanged introductions before ushering the detectives into the parlor, Alec at their heels. At their entrance, the entire room fell silent, whether from the appearance of Alec or the two officers, Alec couldn't be sure.

Wilson introduced Alec, then the detectives to the group, before going around the room tossing out the names of the dozen people standing or sitting in clusters of two or three. Alec lost count of who was who, but a dark-haired young woman in a black skirt and white

Oxford button-down shirt captured his attention as she stacked glasses and plates on a tray.

The young woman hoisted the tray to her shoulder and turned to leave the room, giving Alec his first full view of her face. Even with her eyes focused on the floor, there was no mistaking the mass of curly black hair. Her ponytail brushed her shoulders as she walked. Isabella Montoya, the woman who had kept him sane during his last tour of duty.

Alec didn't follow Isabella out of the room, even though he wanted to. Heloise had mentioned Isabella was her housekeeper and cook, so Alec assumed his aunt had mentioned him to Isabella a time or two. What Isabella didn't know was that Alec knew her much better than as his great-aunt's housekeeper. And Isabella knew Alec too, knew his innermost thoughts—not as Alec, but as his best friend and former commanding officer, Jay Thomas.

What a tangled mess we weave, when first we practice to deceive. Shakespeare sure hit that right on the head. Alec wished he'd never agreed to step in as his major's scribe, penning handwritten letters on Jay's behalf to Isabella, Jay's supposed sweetheart back home. Part of the reason he hadn't come to visit Heloise in the six months he'd been discharged from the Army had been to avoid meeting Isabella face to face. But with his aunt's death, he'd had no choice but to return to Twin Oaks. With any luck, he'd be in and out without Isabella discovering he had been the man behind the words that had wooed her—and fallen in love with her himself.

"Now that everyone's been introduced, Detective Mullins would like the floor." Wilson stood near the mantel with the detectives on his right. The room quieted as the attorney moved to stand at the edge of the crowd, leaving Mullins to come front and center.

"I understand each of you here is related to Heloise Stratman Thatcher." Mullins surveyed the gathering, her eyes resting on each person briefly. "I'm sorry for your loss."

A rotund man with thinning hair half raised his hand. "When can we bury the old girl? It's already been more than a week since she died."

"I don't know when the coroner will release Ms. Thatcher's body," Mullins replied in an even tone.

"Have they determined why she died?" asked a middle-aged woman seated on the couch.

"That's why we're here." Mullins spoke crisply. "We have a cause of death."

CHAPTER 2

❄

Isabella stacked the last of the cups and plates in the dishwasher, bone tired after the physically demanding and emotionally challenging day.

Shelia rinsed the last platter, then drained the sink. "Anything else I can do before I leave? I'm meeting Tom to pick out wedding invitations at his mother's house at seven-thirty, but I can stick around if you need me."

Isabella hugged her friend. "I can finish up. Don't keep your handsome fiancé waiting."

"It's good for a man to wait for his girl every once in a while—makes him more appreciative when she shows up." Shelia grinned as she pulled off her apron and handed it to Isabella.

Isabella hugged the apron to her chest as the finality of Miss Heloise's death hit her afresh. Tears threatened to spill down her cheeks again. "I sure didn't think when I took this job to help my mom that I would still be working here years later. But Miss Heloise made it seem like more than a cleaning and cooking job—she encouraged me to go to school and let me work flexible hours to fit in my classes." She sighed. "I'm going to miss her and this house."

Shelia put her hand on Isabella's shoulder. "You'll be okay. You only have a few more classes to finish your degree, right?"

"Yes, I have two more to go next semester, then I'll graduate in May." Isabella used her own apron to wipe the tears off her cheeks. "Now, shoo. It won't take me long to finish tidying up the kitchen."

Shelia waved goodbye as she slipped out the back door. Ten minutes later, Isabella had the kitchen spotless. Satisfied all was as it should be, she tossed her apron and Shelia's down the laundry chute before shrugging into her coat.

"Isabella?"

"Yes?" She turned to see Mr. Wilson standing in the middle of the kitchen. "Did you need something?"

"I'm afraid there's been a rather unexpected development." The older gentleman's eyes held sadness.

She'd always liked the lawyer, who had treated Miss Heloise with such kindness and respect. "Oh?"

"The police are here."

Isabella frowned. "Is something wrong?"

"I don't know how else to say this but straight out. Heloise was poisoned."

She gasped. "Poisoned?" She pressed her hand to her mouth to steady herself.

Mr. Wilson took a step toward her, his gaze intent. "That's what the medical examiner said."

"But how? Was it an accidental overdose? She did take a lot of medications." Surely it had to be an accident, because otherwise…she didn't want to think about the alternative.

"They haven't determined the cause of the poisoning or even what exactly it was." He shook his head. "I can hardly believe it."

"That's terrible. Poor Miss Heloise." Inconsolable grief assailed her at the thought of her employer ingesting poison. She gripped the kitchen counter to steady herself.

"The detectives have asked everyone to gather in the living room."

With effort, she maintained her composure. "Do you need me to serve coffee?"

"No, you've done enough serving for today." Mr. Wilson regarded her steadily. "The detectives want to question everyone who knew Heloise. Would you please come back to the parlor so we can get started?"

"Of course." Isabella rehung her coat and followed Mr. Wilson out of the kitchen. A question looped in her mind. What if the poisoning wasn't an accident?

❄

ALEC SNAGGED A CHAIR BEHIND THE CROWD OF RELATIVES. WILSON entered the room, followed by Isabella, who slipped behind the sofa to stand with her hands loosely clasped.

At their entrance, Detective Mullins cleared her throat. "Because there are unanswered questions about the death of Ms. Thatcher, we must ask each of you not to leave town."

A man sporting a fat mustache jumped to his feet. "Just how long is this investigation going to last? I have business to attend to."

A woman with salt-and-pepper hair snorted. "Now, Dean, it's nearly Christmas. You can't possibly have that much business this time of year."

Dean huffed. "There's a lot you don't know about what I do, Natalie." He turned toward the detectives. "This is our second trip here in just over a week, so I don't see why we have to stick around because some hick medical examiner suspects an old woman was poisoned."

Detective Mullins raised her eyebrows. "I'll be sure to tell Dr. Bradshure what you think of her medical prowess. But you bring up something I want to clarify—you were here last week? All of you?"

Natalie spoke up. "All of us, except for Alec, came to celebrate Heloise's birthday."

"You can say it's a command performance each December 13," chimed in a man with an impeccably groomed goatee.

Alec pegged his age as in the seventies. Every year, Alec had received an invitation to Aunt Heloise's birthday, but being stationed mostly overseas during his decade in the Army meant he hadn't made a single celebration.

"What do you mean by command performance?" Detective Talbot asked.

"What Charlton alluded to," a stocky middle-aged woman said, "is the fact that Heloise made it very clear that if we didn't come, she would cut us out of her will."

"Janet, that's not entirely true," Charlton replied. "What my dear cousin means is Heloise encouraged us to come. After all, since she never married, we were the only family she had."

"So everyone in this room, with the exception of Alec Stratham, was here with Ms. Thatcher on December 13." Mullins circled her gaze around the room as her partner jotted down something in his notebook.

The group murmured their agreement.

"I see." Mullins exchanged a look with Talbot. "Mr. Wilson has assured me there's plenty of room for you all to stay in this house, if accommodations are needed while we conduct the investigation."

"We'll have to stay here," a rail-thin woman said. "I had already inquired about getting a room at a hotel in town, but everything's full because of Christmas."

"Then by all means, stay here." Wilson shrugged as he glanced around the room. "I'm sure Isabella would be glad to help get everyone settled after the detectives leave."

Alec wasn't sure that was true, but he couldn't see Isabella's face to ascertain her feelings on the matter. The young woman stood in the shadows behind Mr. Wilson's chair, as if trying to blend into the patterned wallpaper.

"How long will we have to stay?" Natalie echoed the earlier question.

"At least until we determine how Ms. Thatcher encountered the poison that killed her," Mullins said.

"Surely it was an accident, because if it wasn't..." Natalie's voice trailed off.

Alec finished the thought for her. "Then someone murdered Aunt Heloise."

CHAPTER 3

❄

Isabella smoothed the quilt on the last bed prepared for the houseguests. Her shoulders drooped with fatigue. She couldn't remember a time when she felt more tired.

"Aren't you finished yet?"

Isabella bottled up a sigh and turned to face Lorna with a tight smile. "All ready for you, Ms. Hemes." She moved to the door as Lorna waltzed in and plopped a small overnight bag at the foot of the bed.

"You can bring up a tray for me in the morning, just black coffee—make sure it's piping hot—and two pieces of toast, lightly buttered."

Isabella managed not to roll her eyes at the woman's command. Mr. Wilson had asked her to do what she could to make their stay comfortable. However, that did not include running up and down the stairs with breakfast trays. "Breakfast will be served buffet-style in the dining room from eight until ten."

"Really, I don't know how Heloise put up with such insubordination." Lorna flung her coat onto a chair.

"You're welcome to bring a tray to your room if you prefer to eat here." Isabella offered a small smile, then exited the room, pulling the door closed with a soft click instead of slamming it like she wanted to.

Lorna wasn't the only relative demanding extras. Janet had wanted the blue bedroom, which had already been claimed by Charlton. The remaining male relatives, with the exception of Alec, had grumbled about being put in the smaller, third-floor bedrooms, while the females had all requested breakfast trays like Lorna. Isabella had politely reiterated the buffet as the only option.

Descending the staircase, Isabella mentally reviewed the contents of the refrigerator and pantry to pull together a morning menu. She would need to replenish with a run to the grocery store tomorrow but not having any idea how long everyone would be staying made coming up with a more extended menu difficult.

"Isabella?"

She jumped, swallowing a cry at the last moment as Alec materialized at the bottom of the stairs. "You startled me."

"I'm sorry—I didn't mean to." He waited while she came down the last few stairs. "Everyone settled in?"

She nodded. "I was just considering what we had on hand for breakfast, as I wasn't expecting overnight guests."

"I don't think anyone blames you for the situation."

She snorted. "If that's what you think, then you really don't know these people." *And at this moment, I wish I didn't either.*

"I don't." Alec leaned against the banister. "I haven't met any of them before today."

"How's that possible?" She tried to discern his expression in the dimly lit hallway but couldn't make out his features. "You're her great-nephew—didn't you live with her for a time?"

"One summer when I was a teenager. She took me in for a time after my parents were killed in an automobile accident."

"I'm so sorry. Miss Heloise didn't mention the circumstances of your visit." With a large, boisterous family of her own, she couldn't imagine having no close relatives.

"Thank you. Aunt Heloise was a godsend. She gave me space to grieve but didn't let me mope about on my own either."

Isabella caught a flash of white as Alec grinned.

"She had a list of honey-dos a mile long, so I painted and sanded and swept and weeded and fixed things all summer long." He paused. "She also encouraged me to talk about my mom and dad."

"She spoke of you often." She blinked back tears at recalling evenings spent with Miss Heloise by the fire in the smaller front parlor, Isabella with her schoolbooks and her employer with her letter writing. "She wrote you often and sometimes read your letters out loud to me." Isabella didn't add that she had developed a harmless crush on the tales Heloise had spun about Alec, even though her heart had belonged to Jay at the time.

Alec moved a step closer. "There's something I should tell you."

"Isabella!"

She jumped as Titus appeared on the landing. "Do you need something?"

"Of course I need something." The man fisted his hands on his hips. "Why isn't the heat on? The radiator in my room is still ice cold."

"I must have forgotten to turn on the one in your room." She put her foot on the bottom stair, but Alec stayed her ascent with a hand on her shoulder.

"I'll do it. I should head up to bed and you've had a very long day."

Relief at not having to climb two flights of stairs flooded her, along with a warmth that snuggled down into her toes. "Thank you."

Alec moved past her and up the stairs. "I'll see you in the morning."

His words reminded her of the Jay who wrote her those beautiful letters. Isabella's mind churned all the way to her carriage house apartment with thoughts of a handsome former Army captain's kindness.

❄

Friday, December 21

The image of Isabella's exhausted face from the night before propelled Alec to hurry down the back stairs in the predawn hour. With any luck, he'd beat Isabella to the kitchen. His shoulders relaxed as he entered the darkened room. He'd start making coffee, then see what could work for breakfast. They would have to get supplies in soon if the police insisted everyone stay beyond today. Maybe Alec could squeeze in a trip to town this morning.

The back door opened and Isabella entered, bringing with her a blast of cold air and a swirl of snow. So much for his getting a head start on the morning meal for everyone.

"I see it's still snowing," Alec said.

At his voice, Isabella jumped, dropping the keys on the floor. "You startled me." She hit a light switch and bathed the kitchen in brightness. "What are you doing up so early?"

"Old Army habit—we always had to rise before the sun." He helped her out of her coat. Wilson mentioned Heloise let Isabella live in the carriage house as part of her wages, so she hadn't far to walk to work.

"Miss Heloise said you'd been recently discharged." She went to the sink and filled a large percolator with water.

"Yes, after being in the Army for ten years." Alec opened the fridge. "And I learned pretty quickly that there's only one person in charge at a time. Tell me what you want me to do, since this household is under your command."

Isabella laughed. "I'm the general, huh?"

Alec met her eyes. "Yes, ma'am." He gave her a cocky salute just to see if he could tease another smile.

Her whole face beamed at him, tugging at his heart with her beauty. "All right then. Let's get to work."

For the next two hours, Alec followed her directions as if she were his old drill sergeant, never questioning, just obeying as quickly and as competently as he could. At eight o'clock, he lit the burners under the chafing dishes on the sideboard in the dining room as Isabella double checked the food.

"All set." She put her hand on her hip. "You know, you're not a bad assistant."

He waved his hand in a flourish and bent over in a bow. "My pleasure to serve you, milady." That brought another smile to her lips. He could get used to seeing that.

"Come on, I'm starving." Isabella turned to exit the dining room.

"But the food's in here." Alec hurried after her when she merely beckoned with her hand for him to come along.

Back in the kitchen, she pulled two foil-covered plates from the oven. "I made us something special."

She put the plates on the small table in the breakfast nook, then poured two cups of coffee from a small carafe by the stove. "How do you take your coffee?"

"Black."

She grabbed silverware and joined him at the table.

He unwrapped his plate: two eggs-in-a-toad with two crisp slices of bacon. "This looks incredible." He eyed her. "How did you do this without my noticing?"

She laid her napkin on her lap. "A cook never reveals her secret."

"Would you mind if I prayed?" At her headshake, he said a short prayer of thanksgiving for the morning meal.

They ate in silence for a few minutes.

"You were with the Army's 2nd Battalion, 198th Combined Arms Battalion, in Iraq?"

He nodded.

"You might have known my, um, ex-fiancé, Jay Thomas? He was a major in that battalion."

Alec slowly chewed the food in his mouth, thankful for the excuse to pause before answering her. So much depended on what he said. "Yes, I know Jay." Alec drew in a breath. Now or never. "In fact, I—"

Janet burst through the swinging door, her robe billowing as she skidded into the kitchen. Her mouth opened and closed with no sound coming out.

Alec rose and headed toward her. "Janet? Are you okay?"

The woman shook her head, her eyes darting around the kitchen.

Isabella approached Janet. "Why don't you sit down and tell us what's the matter?" She slipped her arm around Janet's shoulders, guiding her to the kitchen table.

Alec stood back to let Isabella console the older woman. Janet's shuffled steps drew Alec's attention to her fuzzy bunny slippers on the wrong feet.

Once Janet sank into a chair, Isabella sat beside her, patting the woman's limp hand. "Can you tell us what's gotten you so upset?"

Janet twitched her head up and down in a semblance of a nod. Alec frowned. He'd seen members of his unit make the same kind of jerky movements, usually associated with shock.

"He's, he's." Janet licked her lips, then tried again. "He's not moving."

Isabella shot Alec a look over Janet's slumped form. "Who's not moving?"

"Dean." Janet started to wail. "He's dead!"

CHAPTER 4

❄

"Which room was Dean in?" Alec had his hand on the swinging kitchen door before Isabella could process what Janet had blurted out.

"He's two down from you on the third floor." Isabella turned back to Janet. "Is Dean in his room?"

"No." Sobs shook Janet's body.

"Then where is he?" The command in Alec's voice spoke of years of leadership.

Janet blinked. "He's in the study."

Alec headed out the door without another word.

Isabella pushed a tissue box toward Janet. "What was he doing in the study?" Miss Heloise had kept the door locked, and Isabella hadn't been inside the study to clean for several weeks.

Janet grabbed some tissues and dabbed at her eyes. "I don't know. He sent me a text asking me to meet him there at seven-forty-five, but I overslept. When I arrived, he was lying on the floor, not moving."

Alec returned to the kitchen, his features unreadable.

"What did you find?" Isabella blurted out before Alec could say anything.

"He's dead." He paused. "I've called the police, who told me to lock the study door, but I can't find the key. Do you know where it is?"

"The key wasn't in the lock?" Isabella wrinkled her brow. "Miss Heloise kept a set of house keys in her bedside table." She rose. "I'll fetch them for you."

Alec waved her back to her seat. "No need. I'll run up and get them. We need to keep everyone out of the study until the police arrive."

A shiver inched its way down Isabella's spine. "Why? How did Mr. Sledge die?"

"He was stabbed in the heart," Janet said, her eyes on the floor. "With Heloise's antique letter opener."

Isabella met Alec's gaze and saw the truth of Janet's statement in them before he nodded crisply.

"I'll be back as soon as I've locked the door." Alec slipped out of the room.

First Miss Heloise, then Mr. Sledge. Murdered. Nothing out of the ordinary happened in Twin Oaks. People still talked about the time when the former mayor drove his old truck over the flower beds in the Kitty Tompkins Park next to City Hall after having a glass of champagne at his sixtieth birthday bash—and that was twenty years ago.

Isabella turned back to Janet, who appeared to have calmed down. "When did Mr. Sledge text you?"

Janet blew her nose, then fished out her phone from her robe's pocket. "Last night after everyone retreated to their rooms."

"And he didn't say why he wanted to meet you in the study?"

Janet sighed. "No, just that he had something of interest to tell me."

Isabella changed the subject. "How exactly was everyone related to Miss Heloise? I asked her after this year's birthday gathering but she only said something about family trees needing pruning."

Janet frowned. "That doesn't sound like Heloise."

"Over the past year, she'd been going through all the family papers."

Janet cocked her head. "What do you mean?"

"She'd been working her way through those old trunks in the attic for years." Isabella wasn't sure she should be telling Janet about her employer's fixation on the past. However, the older woman appeared sufficiently distracted by the conversation, so Isabella pressed on. "I always thought she enjoyed reading about her ancestors. But she never really did anything other than list the contents of each box or trunk in a notebook. Then I'd haul it back to the attic and bring her another one. About eight months ago, she started going through the remaining boxes at a faster clip and making piles in the study."

"Sounds like she found something that caught her interest. Any idea what that might have been?" Janet's voice sounded casual, but her tense shoulders told another story.

"I don't know. Miss Heloise didn't share her findings with me." Strictly true. Isabella resisted the urge to shift in her seat at the lie of omission. She always strove to be truthful in all endeavors, and parsing the truth so closely made her uncomfortable.

Alec returned to the kitchen, followed by Detective Mullins, who wore another navy pantsuit and a scowl. Isabella rose and walked to the kitchen sink. Better make more coffee. She had a feeling they would need gallons of it to get through the next few hours.

❆

ALEC ROTATED HIS SHOULDERS AND SHOOK OUT HIS HANDS. How quickly one got out of practice. Standing in one place for less than an hour cramped his muscles. He'd intercepted Titus at the foot of the stairs, and decided to stand guard in front of the study door rather than risk someone contaminating the crime scene by entering the room as he went in search of the key.

Detective Mullins had already been en route to the house when Alec's 911 call went through, and more police had arrived soon after. The place swarmed with plain clothes and uniformed cops, who shuttled Alec out of the way with barely a word of thanks for his efforts. Alec volunteered to take over coffee duty so Isabella could supervise the dining room, where the police assembled the other relatives.

The percolator bubbled, and he poured the steaming liquid into a carafe, started another pot, then carried the fresh brew to the dining room. A uniformed officer opened the door when he approached, then closed it behind Alec.

"I can't believe he's dead." A slender woman with tight curls filled her plate with a tiny spoonful of scrambled eggs and one small serving of fresh fruit. No wonder she looked anemic, if that's how she usually ate.

Alec took the carafe to the sideboard, placing it beside the other one. A quick check revealed it still had a little coffee in it, so he picked it up and turned to the table where nearly all the guests sat. "Anyone need a refill?"

Several people nodded, and Alec went around filling cups as the conversation continued.

"I heard Janet found him, poor thing," the slender woman continued. "She's lying down in her room plum exhausted."

"Lewis refused to come down when he heard the news." Titus slathered butter on a piece of pumpkin-chocolate chip bread.

"That's not too surprising—I guess they were the closest related." Charlton held up his cup to signal Alec, who poured the last of the coffee into it.

"How were they related again?"

Alec didn't see who had asked the question.

"Lewis and Dean were first cousins—Lewis' father and Dean's mother were siblings," Charlton said. "I guess we're all cousins of a sort. Well, except for Alec here." The older man smiled but something about the gesture reminded Alec of a crocodile's grin. "Alec had the closest claim on Heloise as her great-nephew."

Everyone looked in his direction.

"That's true." Natalie gave him an appraising glance. "You have the most to gain from Heloise's death. Although you do realize your lineage is rather sullied."

Alec blinked at her, but before he could ask what she meant, the thin woman laughed. "My dear, you have such old-fashioned views!" The woman waved her hand around. "No one of Alec's generation cares that his great-grandmother never married his great-grandfather, probably because he died before they could make things official."

Alec frowned. His great-grandparents weren't married? With his own parents dying when he was a teenager—and their parents already dead—he never thought much about his relatives beyond Great-Aunt Heloise.

The door opened and Detective Talbot entered. "If I can have everyone's attention, please." He waited a beat for the room to quiet. "We will begin interviewing everyone shortly. Wait in here until you're called."

"Would you please tell us what is going on?" Charlton smoothed down his goatee with his fingers. "We've been told Dean has died but little beyond that."

"He was murdered, Mr. Woods."

At the detective's stark words, someone gasped.

"But who would do such a thing?" Natalie asked, her hand fluttering to her throat.

"How was he killed?" Titus's voice overrode Natalie's query.

"All we can say is that he was murdered. We'll know more after the medical examiner is finished." Talbot turned to go, his hand on the door knob. "As to who would commit such a crime? That's what we're going to find out."

Alec took the opportunity of the detective leaving to follow him out and down the hall to the kitchen with the empty carafe in hand. Two murders in less than two weeks was highly unusual, to say the least.

He rinsed out the carafe, then filled it with more coffee.

"Oh, good. More coffee." Isabella scrubbed a skillet in the sink.

His heart did a little kick in response but he tried to keep his face impassive. No sense grinning like an idiot just because he got to talk to a pretty girl.

A pair of cops entered the kitchen from the back door, stamping snow off their feet. The taller of the two nodded at Isabella and Alec before exiting the kitchen.

Alec turned to Isabella, drawing in a breath and his courage. "There's something I need to tell you."

Isabella put the skillet in the dish drainer. "What's up?" She moved to the pantry. "I think there's disposable cups in here with lids. We can set up a coffee station in the hallway for the police. It's still snowing out there, so I imagine some hot coffee would be welcome."

"Sure, that sounds good." He followed her over to the large pantry. "But there's something you need to know. About Jay."

Her head popped up and she frowned. "What about Jay?"

"It's that, well, we were comrades in Afghanistan." This was harder than he thought it would be. *Come on, Alec! Just tell her.* "The fact is, he used to talk to me about you."

She dropped her eyes, but not before he caught the sheen of tears. What an idiot he was. Of course she would be sad and probably embarrassed by Jay's rejection. Not for the first time, Alec wanted to punch his former commanding officer in the jaw for the callous way he'd treated Isabella. How had Alec not seen the man for who he really was?

"What did he say?" Her voice sounded small and unsure.

Without thinking about it, Alec reached out and touched her arm. "He always had nice things to say about you." True, as far as it went. Alec would never tell Isabella how Jay had laughed about her naivete in believing all the things Alec had written on Jay's behalf, how amusing Jay had found the fact that Isabella had fallen in love with him through his letters. "I'm sorry how things ended."

She swiped a hand across her face and his heart twisted. He wanted to gather her in his arms and kiss away her tears, but he had to tell her about his part in the deception first. And she might not forgive him when she heard the whole story. "Yeah, well, I guess I shouldn't be surprised he'd dump me in a text." She raised her eyes to meet his. "He didn't sound like the man who wrote those beautiful letters. Granted, the text was only a couple of lines, but still, it was almost as if someone else had penned the words that made me fall in love."

Openings didn't get any better than this. Alec shot up a prayer, then took the plunge. "Maybe that's because he didn't."

"What do you mean?" She grabbed the package of hot beverage cups from a shelf.

He took a step back to let her exit the pantry. "Maybe those weren't Jay's words in those letters."

She frowned at him. "You mean he plagiarized someone else's love letters? From what I learned about him afterwards, that wouldn't surprise me."

Her comment confused him, and she must have seen it on his face.

"Before I got the text, I called his cell to see when he was coming over." She raised her eyebrows. "A woman answered, said she was his wife. Turns out they've been married for a month, engaged for a year before that—all the while, he's writing me these soul-revealing letters. She said she knew about the letters and wasn't I a fool for believing Jay would be interested in a little, well, I won't tell you what she called me, but it wasn't nice."

Alec took a step back as if he'd been punched in the gut. Jay had sure pulled the wool over his eyes as well, as he'd not mentioned being engaged, then married, when he'd begged Alec to help him woo Isabella, whom Jay said he'd met on a blind date set up by a mutual friend. How could he have been so stupid as to believe anything Jay said? He'd known his superior's reputation as a man about town, but had been completely taken in by the other man's military acumen and façade of friendship.

"I'm so sorry, Isabella." Alec straightened his shoulders. "I wish I could have stopped him."

"How could you? He was your superior officer—I'm sure he didn't tell you the whole story."

"Ms. Montoya?"

Alec turned around to see a policewoman at the kitchen door.

"The detectives request your presence in the interview room."

"Okay." Isabella set the cups on a tray that held the coffee carafe, creamers, sweeteners, and plastic spoons. "I'll just take these to the front hall on my way."

As she left, Alec mentally slapped himself on the forehead. He should have simply said what he'd done instead of wandering around the topic like a man lost in the desert. Now bringing it up again would be awkward. Even worse, Isabella might not even listen to him, since he'd blown his chance to come clean.

CHAPTER 5

Isabella arranged the coffee on a side table, then accompanied the policewoman to the front parlor. The room had an empty feel with only three people to occupy its vast space. Outside, snow still fell, the gray sky muffling the light from the windows, leaving the room in a gloom that a few lamps tried to penetrate.

She reached for the overhead light switch.

"Leave it off, please." Detective Talbot beckoned her to join him and his colleague in the back of the room where they had pulled three chairs in a semi-circle. "Have a seat."

Isabella tamped down her nervousness as she slid into the empty chair. Stories her mother told of Mexican police dragging her grandfather out of his bodega for not wanting to pay for protection flooded her mind. The police captain simply shot her grandfather in the head in the middle of the street. Her grandmother managed to find an American sponsor for her only daughter, Isabella's mother, who came to the United States as an eight-year-old. Isabella's grandmother and uncles still lived in Mexico, but Isabella's mother became an American citizen. However, her love of her new country couldn't quite overcome her distrust of law enforcement, and she'd passed along her wariness to her children.

"Ms. Montoya, you've been Ms. Thatcher's housekeeper for how many years exactly?" Detective Talbot poised his pen above a notepad as he waited for her answer.

Isabelle willed her heartbeat to slow. This wasn't the Mexican police. These detectives were after whoever killed Miss Heloise and Mr. Sledge. Somehow Isabella doubted there were two killers loose—the deaths had to be connected. She brought her attention back to the detectives. "I've been working for Miss Heloise since I was a senior in high school. That was eight years ago."

Detective Mullins nodded. "When did you move into the carriage house apartment?"

"The summer after I graduated from high school." Isabella reminded herself to only answer the question asked and not volunteer more information. That's what her attorney uncle on her father's side had told her more than once when relating stories from his own practice.

"And your family lives in Gilbert, Virginia, isn't that right?" Detective Mullins said in a caustic tone that raised the hackles on Isabella's neck.

"Yes."

"You come from a rather large family, do you not?" Detective Mullins consulted her notebook, but Isabella suspected it was for show—this woman knew exactly what she wanted to say without referring to notes. "You're the oldest of eight, and your father hasn't been able to work since an on-the-job accident three years ago."

Isabella said nothing, since the detective hadn't asked a question. Inside, she seethed at the implied slur on her family. So they were poor and lived in a two-bedroom apartment in a less-than-desirable part of town. That didn't mean they were criminals. They made ends meet. Much of her own wages went to help out at home.

Detective Talbot smiled at her, but Isabella wasn't fooled by the gesture. "It must have been a godsend to work for Miss Heloise in this big mansion."

Again, Isabella didn't reply. A sliver of unease snaked down her spine, but she kept a pleasant expression on her face.

"Did you know that you're named in her will?" If Detective Mullins had been aiming to shock Isabella, she hadn't succeeded.

"Yes." Isabella had argued with Miss Heloise about the older woman's intention to add Isabella to her will. Honesty compelled her to add, "I mean, Miss Heloise mentioned she was going to, but I don't know if she did."

Detective Talbot pounced on her statement. "So you expected to benefit from Ms. Thatcher's death?"

Isabella didn't try to stop the tears that filled her eyes. "No, I didn't expect to benefit. How can one benefit from the death of someone you love?"

The two detectives exchanged a glance. A cell phone chimed, and Detective Mullins pulled out her phone to glance at the screen. A look of satisfaction crossed her face. "We have a cause of death for Ms. Thatcher."

Isabella held her breath as the detective returned her phone to her pocket.

"She was poisoned with digitalis."

"Isn't that some sort of heart medicine?" Isabella dredged up an old memory of one of her father's aunts who needed to take digitalis to regulate her heart rhythm.

"It is, but this form was unrefined, which means it was most likely ingested in its natural state." Detective Mullins leaned forward, her eyes boring into Isabella's. "Are there any foxglove plants on the property?"

Isabella blinked. The detective wanted to talk about gardening at a time like this? "Well, yes. I planted some along the flower beds last spring. Miss Heloise read about foxglove being a good deer deterrent. I don't think it worked because the deer still ate her begonias and pansies."

"You knew where to find foxglove?" Detective Talbot pressed.

"As I said, I planted it along the back border of the flower beds last spring." Her unease grew stronger, but she straightened her spine and willed her body to project confidence, not fear.

Detective Talbot snapped his notebook closed. "That's all for now."

Isabella got to her feet and left the room, her mind regurgitating the strange conversation. The salient fact that someone had deliberately poisoned Miss Heloise with digitalis hadn't escaped her. She wasn't sure how fast digitalis worked, but she had a feeling that she would find out soon enough.

❄

ALEC CHOPPED CARROTS, THE RHYTHMIC MOTION SOOTHING AS HE WENT over the conversation with Isabella again in his mind.

"What are you doing?" The object of his musings stood beside the counter, her lips turned down in a frown.

"Chopping carrots. I saw leftover chicken in the fridge and figured we could throw together a chicken salad for lunch." He scraped the carrots into a bowl and started on the next one.

"That sounds good." She didn't move, her eyes focused on the movement of his knife as he cut the vegetable into small pieces.

"Are you okay?" He emptied the cutting board into the bowl, and started on the last two carrots.

"Yes. No." She sighed. "The detectives just told me I'm named in Miss Heloise's will, and that she died of digitalis poisoning from ingesting foxglove leaves, I guess."

"Where would someone get foxglove?" Alec brought the washed grapes over to the counter and started slicing them in half for the salad.

Isabella replied, but her voice was inaudible.

"Sorry? What did you say?" He leaned closer.

"I planted foxglove in the flower garden last spring. Miss Heloise thought it would keep the deer from eating her flowers. But it didn't. The deer ate the flowers anyway."

"How would someone get foxglove in December? Wouldn't the leaves turn brown or something?" Alec kept his tone conversational, but he didn't like hearing Isabella had planted foxglove. His stomach flipflopped at the red flag that surely raised with the detectives.

"They will eventually, but we've had a rather warm fall. It only started getting cold last week. The leaves would have still likely been green and on the plant."

Alec finished slicing the grapes. "What else did they ask?"

"About my family." She popped a grape into her mouth.

"What about your family?" Alec had to tread carefully, or he'd give away that he knew a lot about her family from their correspondence. Then again, maybe that would be a good thing, and force him to confess his duplicity.

"They knew about my father's accident and where they live." She pulled the cooked chicken from the fridge. "I don't see why that matters. My family met Miss Heloise a few times when they came to see me."

That amount of background digging sounded like the police were looking at Isabella as a potential suspect. Whether or not she saw it, having a needy family and a rich employer who left her something in her will spelled motive. Isabella's residence in the carriage house apartment gave her proximity to commit the crime. "You don't think they consider you a suspect, do you?"

"Because I planted the foxglove?" Isabella tore the chicken from the bones, adding the meat to the bowl.

"No, because you are a beneficiary in Heloise's will." Alec kept his voice as neutral as possible. The idea that Isabella killed Heloise was downright preposterous, but that didn't mean the police would agree with his assessment.

"But everyone here is a beneficiary. That's why they all come every year to celebrate Miss Heloise's birthday. She made it very clear she would cut out any relative who missed it without a compelling reason." Isabella gathered up the chicken bones and deposited them into the trash can.

"That's true." Alec added chopped onion to the mixture, then fetched the mayonnaise from the fridge. "I'm sure the police are looking into everyone's background."

"Thanks, I feel better." She smiled.

Alec's heart skipped a beat. *Tell her.* "Isabella, you know our earlier conversation, about Jay and the letters?" He put a spoonful of mayo into the bowl, then stirred the contents.

"Yes?" She shook the salt and pepper shakers over the bowl as he added more mayo.

"The thing is, I—"

Wilson came into the kitchen, followed by the two detectives and three other people dressed in white protective gear. "Ah, there you two are."

"What's going on?" Alec rested the spoon against the side of the bowl as Detective Mullins directed the cops to fan out.

"We're executing a search warrant." Mullins waved her hand at them. "You will need to vacate this area until we've cleared it."

"Can we finish making the chicken salad first?" Alec asked. "It will only take a minute."

Isabella stood frozen beside him. He thought a glimpse of panic crossed her face, but before he could reach for her hand to calm her, Talbot called to his partner. The bench near the back door yawned open, and the detective lifted a pair of gardening gloves with several green leaves still ensnared on the Velcro wrist closure.

One look at Isabella's face told him what would happen next.

"Are these yours, Ms. Montoya?" Mullins spoke in a conversational tone that sent chills down Alec's spine.

Isabella nodded.

"And look at that—foxglove leaves stuck on your gloves." Mullins nodded to her partner.

Isabella stared transfixed at the gloves.

Talbot slipped the gloves and leaves into an evidence bag.

"Isabella Montoya." Detective Mullins stepped forward, her mouth in a grim line. "You're under arrest for the murder of Heloise Thatcher."

CHAPTER 6

"Arresting Isabella for the murder of my aunt is ridiculous." Alec longed to say why he was so certain Isabella couldn't have killed Heloise. From her letters, he knew how much she admired and loved the older woman. Seeing Isabella being led away in handcuffs had pierced his heart.

"I agree." Wilson thinned his lips.

Alec paced in the front parlor. "Of course her gardening gloves might have had foxglove in them—she sometimes weeded the flower gardens for Heloise." He paused. "Although I suppose she hasn't done that in a few months, given it's nearly Christmas."

"Which is why they had to arrest her. It gives credence to their theory."

"Isabella wouldn't—did not—murder my aunt."

Wilson frowned. "I might have given them the motive to arrest Isabella."

Alec halted in his tracks. "You?"

"As the probate attorney for Miss Heloise, the detectives asked me who was mentioned in her will. Since she had signed a new one a few months ago, I knew without reviewing the document that Isabella was listed among the beneficiaries."

Surely that wasn't too surprising, given his aunt's fondness for her housekeeper. "But aren't we all in her will?"

"Yes, but Miss Heloise recently added Isabella into the will, while the rest of you have been in there all along."

"I see." Still, how could anyone believe Isabella capable of murder?

Wilson pulled out his phone. "I'm going to call a criminal lawyer I know. This is out of my area of expertise."

"Good. She shouldn't be alone with the detectives. I'll pay whatever it takes to get that attorney to the jail pronto." Alec could barely wrap his mind around the image of Isabella being read the Miranda warning.

Wilson nodded, then held the phone to his ear. "Don't worry—I know Isabella didn't poison Miss Heloise."

At Wilson's declaration, some of the tension eased from Alec. His stomach grumbled, reminding him that he'd barely had breakfast and it was nearly lunchtime. "I'm going to see if the police have finished searching the kitchen."

Wilson turned away as he spoke into the phone. "Hello?"

Alec hurried along the hallway to the kitchen, which was deserted. The bowl of ingredients for chicken salad, along with the mayonnaise jar, sat undisturbed on the counter. As he mixed in more mayo, he prayed for Isabella. *Please, God, help me to figure out who really killed Heloise and Dean.*

"Good news." Wilson stepped into the kitchen. "David Keener, the attorney I just spoke with, will go as soon as he can to the police station. In the meantime, I'll head over there and see what I can learn about the evidence against her."

"Thank you." Alec dumped the chicken salad into a large serving bowl. "I'll try to find out what the others know during lunch. Since Isabella didn't do it, we must discover who did."

Wilson paused with his hand on the back door. "Be careful. Someone has killed twice so far."

"Thanks for the warning, but after three combat tours in Iraq and Afghanistan, I can take care of myself."

"I have no doubt you're a highly skilled soldier, but please don't underestimate the murderer."

"You can count on that." Once Wilson had gone, Alec concentrated on lunch. The pantry yielded a couple of boxes of fancy crackers, so he put those in a lined basket. Carrots and celery sticks would do for a crudité tray.

When he had finished setting up the simple buffet in the dining room, the other relatives appeared in small groups, as if drawn by an invisible thread at the scent of food. The overall mood had lightened somewhat since the morning's discovery of Dean's body. Alec didn't have to wait long to find out why his cousins were in a happier frame of mind.

Titus grabbed several crackers, then spooned a large helping of chicken salad onto his plate. "I warned Heloise that she was putting too much trust in her housekeeper."

Alec tamped down a harsh response. He'd probably learn more if he appeared to be on their side, so he simply nodded along with the others.

Janet got in line behind Titus. "I wonder what evidence they had to arrest her?"

"They found her gardening gloves hidden in the kitchen with foxglove caught in the Velcro." Charlton wrinkled his nose at the buffet, but still filled his plate.

Alec poured water into goblets on the table and tried not to look like he was listening to their conversation.

"How did you find that out?" Janet's tone held admiration and a touch of envy, as if she would have rather imparted that juicy bit of news. She seemed to have completely recovered from her ordeal of finding Dean's body.

"I overheard a couple of those policemen talking about it." Charlton set his plate down at the head of the table. "I must say this is a paltry luncheon."

"For goodness' sake, Charlton. What did you expect after the housekeeper/cook is hauled off to jail?" Lorna plunked down her plate next to Charlton.

Alec opened his mouth to say something he'd probably regret, but Natalie spoke first.

"But what if she had time to make this? Would you feel safe eating it?" Natalie placed a couple of carrot sticks on her empty plate, then slid into her seat.

"Ah, but she did have time to make the chicken salad." Petty of him to say so, but Alec couldn't resist the dig. Grim satisfaction coursed through his body as everyone turned to stare at him, forks suspended in midair. He tossed off a saucy grin as he put a large spoonful of chicken salad on his plate and joined them at the table. Shaking salt and pepper onto the salad, he forked some into his mouth.

Natalie twittered, her giggle high-pitched and grating. "I see you're not concerned."

Alec paused to wipe his mouth and schooled his features to hide his concern. "Not a bit. I know Isabella wouldn't harm Aunt Heloise."

"The police think otherwise." Charlton pushed his plate away with half of the chicken salad uneaten. "They've arrested her."

"I suppose they'll figure out soon enough she had nothing to do with it. Evidence like you described could have been easily planted by the real murderer." Alec forked salad onto a cracker. "And I think you're all forgetting one important fact."

Eleven pairs of eyes turned his way. "What's that?" Janet asked the question clearly written on everyone's face.

"The police didn't arrest her for the murder of Dean Sledge."

❄

AFTER BOOKING HER—AN EXPERIENCE THAT LEFT HER SHAKEN AND humiliated—the detectives deposited Isabella in a small room with the ubiquitous one-way mirror on one wall, a video camera, and a metal table with three chairs.

The police interrogation room reeked of fresh paint, a scent that always turned Isabella's stomach. She had barely eaten any breakfast, which was a good thing given the churning of her tummy. While she waited alone, she took shallow breaths through her mouth, but the smell coated her tongue.

As the minutes clicked by, Isabella reviewed what had happened over the past twenty-four hours, wondering what clues she was missing. She lingered over her encounters with Alec. Picturing his broad shoulders and gray eyes calmed her.

Forty-five minutes later, the door opened to admit Detectives Mullins and Talbot, who each walked in carrying manila folders. The two sat across from Isabella. Talbot used a remote to start the video recording. He crisply stated the date, time, and those present for the interview. Then he stopped talking and merely waited.

For a full minute—Isabella ticked off the seconds in her head—the detectives allowed the silence to build. Most people would have started talking to fill the awkward quiet, but Isabella was comfortable with silence. As a child, her mother often had them practice sitting quietly, allowing the air to grow heavy with the things unsaid. Her mother called it "preparation" just in case they ever returned to Mexico and had to deal with the police or drug cartels and their intimidation tactics. Isabella always won the silent game—she could outlast even her mother.

"Are you in this country legally?" Detective Talbot crossed his arms and leaned back in his chair, his gaze leveled at Isabella.

This time, Isabella allowed a smile to cross her face. So far, the two were following a script Isabella had been prepared for since childhood. "I am an American citizen, born in this country."

"Do you know why you're here?" Detective Mullins took over the questioning.

"Because you think I killed Miss Heloise." Isabella used what her mother called a subservient voice. The deferential tone showed Isabella wasn't placing herself "above her station" in life. A way to placate those who thought Hispanics needed to stay in a certain place.

"What about your parents?" Talbot asked. "Are they here legally?"

"My mother is a naturalized citizen, and my father was born in America." Isabella was fiercely proud of that fact. Still, it irked her that her legal status would be questioned just because of her Hispanic heritage.

"Did you know Ms. Thatcher mentioned you in her will?"

The way Talbot tightened his shoulders as he asked the question signaled its importance. Isabella chose her words as carefully as if trimming a roast to perfection. "You asked me that earlier and my answer's the same: Miss Heloise said she was changing her will to leave me something."

"When did she tell you that?" Mullins leaned across the table, her hands nearly touching Isabella's clasped fingers.

"A few months ago." Isabella stopped herself from saying anything more. Mr. Wilson would have told the detectives the date on the will, so adding information would only make Isabella look more guilty.

"Did you know what your inheritance would be when Ms. Thatcher died?" Talbot spoke again.

"No." Isabella gave the one-word answer and waited for the follow up. Having to weigh every word was harder than she anticipated. A knock on the door gave her a relief from their scrutiny.

The door opened before the detectives could respond verbally. A uniformed policewoman stood aside to allow a man with horn-rimmed glasses and the curliest brown hair Isabella had ever seen on a man to squeeze past the officer into the small room. "I'm David Keener, Miss Isabella Montoya's attorney. I request an immediate end to this interrogation to confer with my client."

It took every ounce of Isabella's composure not to betray surprise or elation at Mr. Keener's entrance.

"Interview terminated at twelve fifty-three p.m." Talbot punched off the video camera with the remote. Then the detectives gathered their folders and left.

Once the door shut behind them, Mr. Keener took the seat across from Isabella. "Mr. Wilson hired me to represent you. What did you tell them?"

Isabella recounted the questions and her sparse answers.

Keener nodded a few times as he took notes on a yellow legal pad.

When she finished, he tapped the pad with his pen. "Is this your first arrest?"

"Yes." Isabella hoped it would be her last.

"If all my clients were as tight-lipped as you, my job would be a lot easier."

"I did the right thing?"

Keener smiled, a boyish grin that made him look like he was barely out of high school, much less a practicing attorney. "You did splendidly."

"I still can't believe they arrested me." Putting the words out there made her realize all over again how serious the situation was.

Keener met her gaze. "The police are concerned with means, opportunity, and motive, and there was enough to justify your arrest. You told them yourself that you planted the foxglove on Ms. Thatcher's behalf, putting you in the perfect position of knowing where to find—for lack of a better phrase—the murder weapon. To make matters worse, they found foxglove leaves on your gardening gloves."

Isabella shuddered. *Oh, Miss Heloise. Who could have hated you so much as to kill you?*

"As for opportunity, you were in the house, preparing all of Ms. Thatcher's meals, et cetera." Keener ticked off the third item. "And motive. You're named in her new will."

Put so starkly, no wonder she'd been arrested. Had she been in their shoes, she would have arrested herself, but for one vital thing—she didn't do it. "But that applies to all the other relatives, too. I planted that foxglove in the garden last year, and Miss Heloise mentioned it at her birthday gathering a few weeks ago."

Keener straightened. "Who was at that gathering?"

Isabella recited the names of the relatives. "Everyone who was at the house for her funeral, except for Alec Stratman. He wasn't present for her birthday."

Keener scribbled more notes.

"I don't know how long it takes for digested foxglove to poison someone, but anyone would have known where to find it on the property." She thought back to what the detectives had said to her back at the house. "I think it was probably mixed with something else."

"We'll know more once the medical examiner finishes his autopsy report, but with Christmas a few days away, that might take a while. What about motive for the other relatives?"

"Same as mine, isn't it? Everyone came to celebrate Miss Heloise's birthday because they didn't want her to cut them out of the will."

"Tell me about the relatives and how they're related to her."

Isabella rubbed her temple. "Miss Heloise went over the family tree with me before her birthday this year, so I think I have them all straight. They're mostly cousins, expect for Alec Stratman—he's her great-nephew."

"It would be helpful if you wrote down everyone and how they're related." Keener handed her the legal pad and a pen.

"Okay." Isabella turned to a fresh page and started writing.

Great Nephew: Alec Stratman

First Cousin: Charlton Woods

First Cousins, Once Removed: Lorna Hermes, Scott Saunders

First Cousins, Twice Removed: Janet Bothman, Titus Simons, Brad Jones, Gillian Robertson

Second Cousin: Natalie Evens

Third Cousins, Twice Removed: Rachel Montgomery, Lewis Clark, Missy Gainer, Dean Sledge

She handed the page back to Keener.

"I don't remember what all this 'removed' stuff means. Can you explain?" Keener tapped his pencil on the page.

"Sure, I'll try." Isabella tried to find a more comfortable position in the chair. "The way I understand it, 'once removed' means you're one generation farther away. 'Twice removed' is two generations father away."

"So the first cousins, once removed, are closer to Ms. Thatcher than the first cousins, twice removed?"

"That's right."

"But the great-nephew beats all of them for being the closest relative to Ms. Thatcher?" At Isabella's nod, Keener made another notation on the list. "Okay, I'm going to see when we can have an arraignment, so I can get you out of here." He stood and walked to the door. "But don't say another word unless I'm present and say you can."

She agreed as the attorney gathered his things. He rapped on the door and told the police officer to notify the two detectives that he was leaving. Isabella relaxed against the back of the chair for the first time since walking into the room. At least someone was on her side.

CHAPTER 7

*A*lec held the back door open for David Keener to exit ahead of him. The attorney had just arrived after seeing Isabella, so Alec suggested the outside kitchen garden to ensure privacy. With snow threatening to fall, they would likely not be overheard by the others, who had all retreated to their rooms after lunch and appeared not to notice Keener's arrival.

"How long will she be in jail?" Alec ignored the cold as he walked beside the attorney.

"The arraignment is tomorrow morning at nine," Keener said. "Wilson assured me the estate would put up any bail money, and she should be free by noon."

"Can I see her tonight? Bring her anything?" The need to see that Isabella was okay tightened his stomach.

Keener shook his head. "Sorry, visiting hours are over for today. I hope to have Isabella home in time for lunch tomorrow."

"How strong is their case?" Alec wasn't sure if the attorney could share details but that wasn't going to stop him from asking. He needed all the help he could get if he was going to present the police with the real killer of Heloise and Dean.

"You mean besides the trifecta of means, opportunity, and motive?"

Alec winced. "Yeah, apart from that—which, I might point out, is what we all have in common, except for me. I wasn't anywhere near Twin Oaks until yesterday, and I can prove it."

Keener held up his hand. "No one's accusing you—yet. But from the list of those who are named in Ms. Thatcher's will, there are no shortage of suspects. However, it's the physical evidence that led the cops to arrest Isabella."

"The gardening gloves with foxglove leaves." Alec halted. Had the killer known those were Isabella's gloves? Or had the person merely grabbed the most convenient pair of gloves before going out to snip the poisonous plant? He'd forgotten how warm some Virginia autumns could be, keeping outdoor plants green well into December—and this year, keeping the foxglove plants healthy enough to kill Heloise.

"You heard about that?"

Alec nodded. "I was in the kitchen when the detective found the gloves. Did you hear anything about the murder of Dean Sledge?"

"Wilson told me about that. However, the police only questioned Isabella about the death of Ms. Thatcher." Keener rubbed his hands together. "Do you think they're connected?"

"That I don't know, but it seems the most likely scenario—more likely than two murderers killing off members of the same family."

"Tell me about Dean."

Alec related what little he knew about the man and his murder. "All I can say for certain is that Isabella was with me from six a.m. until the body was found."

"And the body was warm when you checked?"

"He couldn't have been dead long." Alec had seen death as a soldier, but touching Dean's still-warm corpse had been an entirely different experience. As a soldier, death was an expected component of life, especially when deployed to dangerous countries. He didn't expect to encounter it in his great-aunt's office.

"Hmm." Keener tucked his scarf around his neck. "I'd concentrate on finding out who could have killed Ms. Thatcher first."

Alec raised his eyebrows. "What makes you think I'll be investigating these deaths?"

Keener smiled. "Because it's obvious that you're in love with Isabella. And any soldier worth his salt is going to fight tooth and nail for the woman he loves."

❄

ALEC HUMMED AS HE PEELED POTATOES. GOOD THING HE'D SPENT LOTS of quality time with an Army lieutenant who loved to cook. Now he tossed the cubed potatoes with garlic, rosemary, and olive oil before dumping them into a roasting pan and sliding it into the hot oven.

With any luck, dinner would bring more than hungry appetites to the table—he could direct the conversation to find out where everyone was in the days leading up to Heloise's death. He'd called a former Army doctor buddy to ask how quickly digitalis works to establish a timeline. Since digitalis could kill within hours if the dose was large enough, all he had to do was ferret out who exactly had access to the house during the time frame in question.

Alec had invited Wilson to join them, as questions were bound to arise about the will and how Dean's death impacted that document. He'd also asked Keener to come, but the attorney declined, noting that his presence as defense counsel for Isabella would likely dampen conversation.

At six on the dot, Alec set the last dish on the table and stood back to admire his handiwork. Roasted potatoes, green beans, roast beef, gravy, and warm crusty rolls—a meal of comfort foods designed to loosen tongues and put the relatives at ease.

"Where'd all this come from?" Scott Saunders pulled out a chair.

"The store." Alec stood at the head of the table in a move designed to both irk Charlton—who had been acting as head of the family—and establish his own status as Heloise's closest relative.

"I meant who cooked it." Scott grabbed a roll and began slathering butter on it.

"I did." Alec waited a beat, still standing behind his chair. "Let's wait for everyone else to arrive before we start."

Scott stuffed part of the roll in his mouth, then gave a thumbs up.

Alec managed not to roll his eyes at the man's manners. Charlton immediately walked toward the chair at the head of the table, but halted in his tracks. Alec offered a smile but didn't budge. The older man huffed, then chose the seat directly to Alec's right.

Soon everyone, including Wilson, had arrived. Alec sat and laid his napkin on his lap. "I'd like to say grace before we eat."

Titus set down the bowl of potatoes with more force than necessary. Alec ignored him and bowed his head without waiting to see if the others would follow suit. "Dear Heavenly Father, thank you for the food before us. Thank you for Heloise and her life. We pray that you will give the police wisdom as they search for her killer and for whoever murdered Dean as well. Amen."

He raised his head, and reached for the platter of sliced beef to pass to Charlton. "I hope you enjoy the meal. It was the best I could do on short notice."

"You made this?" Janet served herself green beans.

"Yes." Alec didn't offer any other explanation. For a while, the talk centered around passing the food and asking for the salt or pepper shakers and butter.

"Wilson, when will Heloise's will be read?" Lorna asked.

"I can read it tomorrow afternoon at two o'clock."

The other relatives murmured their assent to this plan.

Alec used the comment to segue into the conversation he'd planned. "Since I wasn't able to make her birthday party, I was hoping to learn more about Heloise's last days. When was the last time you saw her, Charlton?"

Charlton blotted his mouth with a napkin. "Let's see. I was here for her birthday celebration, as was everyone else at the table, except for you."

"So that's the last time you saw Heloise?" Alec cut his beef and took a bite.

"No." The older man sipped his water. "I'd forgotten my favorite pair of slippers in my room here, and returned the next day to retrieve them."

"That's not quite true, is it?" Titus pointed at Charlton. "I saw you leaving the house on Sunday morning, not Saturday."

Charlton's expression didn't change, but his hand trembled slightly as he picked up his fork. "I'm not sure who you thought you saw, but it wasn't me. I was at home Sunday morning in Harrisonburg."

"Can anyone prove it?" Titus challenged.

"Since I live alone, no." Charlton returned to cutting his meat. "But if you claim to have seen me Sunday morning, then that means you must have been here as well. What were you doing?"

Titus shrugged. "I already told the police I was here Sunday morning around ten a.m. Heloise asked me to stop by when I was going through town on my way to Roanoke, so I did."

"You might have been the last person to see Heloise alive!" Janet put her hand to her mouth. "What did she want and how was she?"

"That's the funny thing. She seemed surprised to see me so soon after her birthday party." Titus frowned, dropping his gaze. "In fact, she was not like her usual self. Something was bothering her, but when I asked her what, she tore a strip off my hide for asking."

"You didn't press her?" Janet said.

Natalie broke into the conversation with a light laugh. "When has pressing Heloise ever made her tell you anything? The woman was always going to do what she wanted to do, regardless of what anyone else thought or suggested."

Alec detected a note of bitterness in her voice. "When did you last see Heloise, Natalie?"

She turned to Alec, amusement dancing in her eyes. "Trying to trip one of us up to get that lovely little housekeeper off the hook for murder?"

With effort, Alec kept his face impassive, and merely regarded her steadily.

"Since I have nothing to hide, I'll indulge you. I haven't been back here since I left around noon on December 14, the day after Heloise's birthday party." Natalie glanced round the table. "Who's next? Alec isn't the only one dying to know who has an alibi and who doesn't."

❄

An hour later, Alec loaded the plates into the dishwasher. He was no closer to finding who had poisoned Heloise than he had been before dinner. The only thing he had was a list of four names who had the opportunity: Charlton, Titus, Lorna, and Janet. All admitted to having been either at the house or nearby on Sunday, December 16.

"That went better than I thought it would." Wilson dumped the cloth napkins into the laundry hamper next to the pantry. "At least we know who had access to this house on the day Heloise died."

Alec put in a dishwashing tab and started the machine. "It doesn't bring us any closer to finding out who killed Heloise."

"It would if we could determine which of those four had a stronger motive than being an heir to her estate."

"During dinner, Janet asked Titus why he skipped a charity event he usually attended," Alec said. "Titus brushed it off, but maybe he's having money troubles."

"I'll see what I can find out about his finances. But there's still the matter of Sledge's death." Wilson leaned back against the counter.

Alec was silent as he rinsed the pot. "Everyone's a suspect for that because we were all in the house when he was killed," he said finally.

"However, you and Isabella give each other alibis."

"True." Alec dried the pot, then wiped down the counters. "You think whoever killed Heloise also killed Dean?"

"That makes the most sense to me."

"The police must not share your view."

Wilson straightened. "The police prefer to work with facts, and the facts, as they see it, point to several suspects. However, Isabella's the only one with hard evidence connecting her to the Heloise's murder.

You and I find that a little too convenient, but the detectives find it compelling enough to arrest her."

"You don't think they'll try to pin Dean's murder on Isabella too?" Alec couldn't bear it if Isabella was arrested for that crime as well.

"No, but that could change once the medical examiner determines a more exact time of death."

Alec sighed. "I don't like it. I have the feeling we're missing something important. I can't figure out the timing. Why kill Heloise now? She just celebrated her ninety-third birthday, and probably wouldn't live to see her ninety-fourth."

"You're forgetting that she changed her will recently."

"That's what got Isabella arrested."

"I think the better question is what else changed between the previous will and the new one." Wilson reached into the inside pocket of his suit coat and withdrew an envelope. "This isn't strictly ethical, but Miss Heloise spoke so highly of you that I think she would have wanted you to have this now."

Alec took the envelope. "What is it?"

The attorney leaned closer and lowered his voice. "A copy of Heloise's will. I think you'll find it very interesting bedtime reading. And now, I'll be off for the night. See you tomorrow afternoon."

Alec walked Wilson to the door, then slipped upstairs to his room. Once inside, he locked the door, sat on the bed, and opened the envelope. He read the contents twice before returning the pages to the envelope. While he didn't have a clear idea as to who killed Heloise and Dean, he had a much better notion as to why Heloise had died.

CHAPTER 8

※

Saturday, December 23

Alec held the small flashlight between his teeth, its beam directed at the small window on the bottom of the gas hot water heater as he followed the instructions to relight the pilot light. With a whoosh, the flame flickered and held. Cranking the temperature gauge back to its normal setting, he turned off the flashlight and got to his feet. At least he'd risen early enough to notice something wasn't right with the hot water in time to fix it before the others awoke. He'd always enjoyed the quiet of the predawn.

With any luck, Isabella would be home in a few hours. He only wished he had better intel to offer on who killed Heloise and Dean. Maybe today, he'd learn the vital piece of information that would crack the case wide open. And maybe he needed to stop thinking life was like a made-for-TV movie.

Climbing the basement stairs, he started to push open the door into the kitchen when he heard someone talking.

"Listen, I said I'd have your money soon."

The lowered voice made identifying the speaker difficult. Alec pressed his ear to cracked door.

"I can't rush probate! It will take a few weeks once the will is read." Another short pause. "I'm sure. Heloise always said she would divide her estate among her relatives. This house alone is worth a fortune. I already have someone interested in turning it into a B&B. The other relatives are as eager to sell as I am."

The caller paced away from the cellar door. Alec eased it open a little bit more to catch a glimpse.

"All right. I'll call you tonight with an update."

Alec waited to see if the person would leave the kitchen, but all he heard were sounds of someone opening cupboards and rattling dishes.

"Titus, you're up early." Charlton's voice easily carried throughout the kitchen.

So Titus owed someone money, a lot of it, by the desperation in his voice as he spoke on the phone.

"Trying to figure out how to make coffee in this place."

"I'd love a cup myself, given there's no hot water. My morning ablutions were decidedly chilly today," Charlton said.

Alec decided that was his cue to enter the kitchen. He pushed through the door, acting surprised at seeing the two men. "Titus, Charlton." He shot a look at the kitchen wall clock, which registered six forty-five. "You're both up early. I haven't started the coffee yet."

"There is no hot water." Charlton stated that as if it were Alec's fault.

"I know. Had a rather chilly shower this morning myself." He grinned at the older man. "But thank goodness it was just the pilot light that had gone out. I relit it, and we'll have hot water again soon."

"That's a relief." Charlton waved his hand around the kitchen. "Any chance of some coffee?"

"Next on my agenda." Alec replaced the flashlight into the kitchen junk drawer, then got out the percolator.

"I'll get out of your way." Titus gave Alec a tight smile before exiting.

"And I'll be in the living room," Charlton said as he swept from the room.

As Alec measured the ground coffee, he sent up another prayer for Isabella's release and the real killer or killers would be uncovered soon.

❄

While David Keener finished up a phone call in his car, Isabella stood in the driveway, relishing the fat snowflakes tumbling around her. Breathing in the crisp air stirred thankfulness for her new-found freedom. The night in jail had been harder than anticipated. The invasion of privacy, constant hum of noise, and coarse talk of the other women had picked at her nerves until Isabella nearly screamed at the guards to throw her into solitary confinement. Reciting the Twenty-Third Psalm under her breath had not only prevented a meltdown, but the muttering also kept the other women away from her.

This morning, the judge granted her bail, which Wilson posted from Heloise's estate. She didn't entirely understand how that was possible, but both attorneys assured her it was legal. She only cared that she was free—at least until the trial. Mr. Keener told her the judge would set the trial date at another court appearance after the New Year.

As she waited for Mr. Keener to accompany her inside the house, she looked up at the home of Miss Heloise had lived in all her life, its Federalist style apparent in the symmetrical windows on either side of the central front door, the semicircular fanlight and decorative crown above the entryway. Snow covered the roofline and dusted the front portico. She'd fallen in love with it the first time she'd seen it—the warm, aged brick nearly glowing in the afternoon sunlight, the sparkling windows with their matching shutters, the oval front parlor, and the arched doorways. When Miss Heloise hired her to clean twice a week, Isabella had enjoyed getting to know the house's decorative swags and garlands that enhanced the simplicity of the architecture. Her love for the house had made Miss Heloise happy. On more than one occasion, Miss Heloise had talked about its history over a cup of tea.

"Ready to go in?" Mr. Keener gestured toward the house just as the door with its beautiful boxwood wreath and bright red bow opened.

Alec stepped out onto the porch, his gaze on her. A sense of homecoming washed over her. Why did she feel like she knew this man so well? Over the past forty-eight hours, she'd thought a lot about the connection with a man she'd heard about for years, but never met until now. Yet the sense that she did know him wouldn't leave her. But with an accusation of murder hanging over her head, she needed to concentrate on clearing her name, not on how a pair of brown eyes warmed her heart.

"From what Wilson told me, I don't think Alec will leave your side." Mr. Keener smiled at her. "He's ready to slay dragons on your behalf."

"My knight in shining armor?" She liked that thought.

"Something like that. Shall we?" Mr. Keener walked beside her as they made their way to the waiting Alec.

"Isabella." Alec extended his hand. "Let's walk in together."

Her stomach did a little flip-flop at the sound of her name on his lips. "Thank you." She accepted the assistance of his firm grip without hesitation. She would need all the strength she could rally to make it through the gauntlet of relatives, one of whom had murdered Miss Heloise and Dean.

Alec tucked her hand through the crook of his arm, and together they entered the house. "It's so good to see you."

Isabella couldn't stop the wide smile that spread over her face. "It's good to see you too."

Once inside, she drew in the cleansing scent of the old house. The familiar aroma of wood polish, the sharp pine of Christmas greenery and the warmth of cinnamon-scented candles welcomed her.

Mr. Keener trailed behind them and closed the door once inside. He muttered something about finding Wilson, leaving the two of them in the foyer alone.

"Have you had lunch?" Alec helped her remove her heavy winter coat Mr. Keener had brought to the jail. In doing so, his hand brushed against her bare neck, setting her skin a tingle. "I could whip up a sandwich for you."

"We went to a drive-thru. Mr. Keener thought it would be best to grab a bite along the way." She had nearly protested the delay in returning home but when her stomach growled at the first whiff of frying beef, she'd seen the wisdom in eating now, rather than later.

When he moved away to hang her garment on the coat tree by the front door, she missed the closeness of standing next to him with her hand on his arm.

Task complete, he turned back to her, his eyes lingering on her face.

Her cheeks warmed under his scrutiny. "Do I have something on my face?"

"No." But he reached up and gently touched her cheek with a featherlight caress anyway. Then his expression sobered. "Isabella, there's something I've been trying to tell you."

She attempted a light laugh, but it came out more like a squeak. The serious look in his eyes pinched her heart. Whatever he had to tell her, it wasn't going to be good.

"I should have told you right away." He glanced around the foyer. "Can we talk in the study?"

Isabella couldn't quite suppress a shudder. "The police have finished with the room?"

"Yes, but I'm sorry. I wasn't thinking that you might not want to be in a room where..." His voice trailed off.

"Where a dead body was discovered," she finished for him. "But you're right—it's probably the most private place in the house."

He crossed the hall and opened the study door, with Isabella at his heels.

Once inside, she glanced around at Miss Heloise's desk now coated with fingerprint dust. A dark stain coated the hard wood floor visible beneath a missing chunk of rug the crime technicians must have cut to preserve as evidence. Isabella turned to Alec. "What did you want to tell me?"

He blew out a breath. "This is harder than I thought. I mean, it shouldn't be, but I'm afraid once you know, you'll not have anything more to do with me."

His rambling sent a shiver down her spine as she sifted through his words to find a meaning that made sense. "I don't understand what you're saying."

Alec ran his hand over his short-cropped hair. "That's because I'm making a mess of things. I'm just going to spit it out: I was your pen pal."

"Pen pal?" Of all the possibilities whirring through her brain at what he might say to her, that wasn't even on her radar. "I don't have a pen pal."

"Yes, you did." His gaze pinned hers with a stare so intense, she couldn't have looked away if she'd wanted to. "You thought you were writing to Jay, but you were really writing to me."

His words penetrated the fog in her brain as if sunlight had pierced through the clouds on an overcast day. "Wait a minute."

She stumbled back a step as snippets of Jay's letters tumbled through her mind. The lyrical images he'd painted of a street market in Kabul. The pain of losing a member of their squad to an IED on an Afghan road. All so very different from the way Jay had spoken during their infrequent Skype chats, where it sometimes seemed as if Jay couldn't remember that he'd written her at all.

She tapped her forefinger on his chest. "You wrote those letters?"

At his nod, Isabella narrowed her eyes as the implication of his words stripped away the veneer. "So this was all some sort of Cyrano de Bergerac thing?"

"No, not like that."

Misery stamped every line of Alec's face, but Isabella ignored his pain, choosing instead to focus on her own. "I think you'd better start at the beginning."

"Jay was my superior officer. At first, he needed a scribe because he'd hurt his right hand during a training exercise and couldn't hold a pen. He said something about your preference for real letters."

She'd begged Jay to send handwritten letters, as if touching the page he had touched with a pen would make him seem closer to her. Theirs had been a whirlwind romance. Though with the clarity of hindsight, she had read more into his words and gestures than he had might have intended.

"When he dictated that first letter, I kept trying not to laugh. It was so stilted and unlike how Jay talked."

How Jay had charmed her on their blind date, smoothing over the awkward moments. They'd only dated for six months when his unit was called up for a twelve-month deployment to Afghanistan and he'd asked her to marry him. She had been enchanted by the idea of receiving letters from her soldier fiancé. Maybe if she'd had time to date other boys in high school, she wouldn't have fallen for what she now saw as Jay's slick talk and handsome face. With her parents pushing her to get the college education they had forgone, she'd had little time for dating in between working and schoolwork.

Alec continued. "He could see by my expression that I thought his letter writing was lame. Jay challenged me to write a better one, so I did. He liked it so much, he sent it. I told him not to, but he didn't listen."

"That was one letter. Why did you continue for so long?" At least her voice hadn't cracked asking that question.

"He showed me your response, then told me to write another letter for him." Alec gave her a half smile. "I should have refused outright, but, well, I was coming up for captain soon, and without my commanding officer's recommendation, I could kiss that promotion goodbye. You know how persuasive Jay can be."

Yes, she did know. Otherwise, she would never have agreed to become engaged to him before his deployment. He'd begged her not to send a soldier off to a war zone without hope that he'd have a girl back home waiting for him. What she hadn't realized was Jay's need to have not just one girl, but multiple ones on his string.

"You wrote letters to me, *love letters*, pretending to be someone else for nearly a year." It did hurt to know that someone other than Jay had read about her hopes and dreams while pretending to care. "The deception didn't bother you?" This time, she hoped he heard the anguish gripping her voice.

"It did, but honestly, after the first couple of letters, I didn't pretend anymore." He took a step closer to her. "Those words? Those were my words, my thoughts, not Jay's." Alec captured her gaze with his own. "The truth is, I fell in love with you through your letters. I didn't want to stop writing to you, even though I knew it was wrong, even though I knew you thought Jay was the man behind the letters. Knowing you were reading *my* letters, writing back to *me*, and thinking about *me as Jay*, was all that kept me going over there some days."

A small part of her sighed with relief that she hadn't truly been in love with Jay after all, but Alec posing as Jay. However, her heart cried out at the pain of Jay's betrayal, fresher now that she knew Alec's part in the deception. Alec, championed by Heloise as such an honorable man, usually in contrast to Jay's character, had perpetuated the charade.

"I'm so, so sorry. I wish I'd have come clean after those first few letters. But I didn't want to risk your cutting off our communication. I tried to tell you yesterday during breakfast but Janet burst in with news of Dean's death before I could." He reached out his hand as if to touch her arm, but let his hand fall back to his side without making contact.

A knock on the closed study door interrupted them. Isabella latched onto the distraction, not wanting to deal with her conflicted feelings about Alec at the moment.

Mr. Wilson opened the door. "Ah, there you two are." He walked over to Isabella. "My dear, I'm so glad you're back."

"Thank you." Isabella drew in a breath to steady her nerves. "It's good to be home."

"Did David tell you about the reading of the will this afternoon?"

Isabella nodded. It took everything in her not to bolt from the room so she could recover her equilibrium in private.

"It's nearly time. We're gathering everyone together in the front parlor." Wilson looked from Alec to Isabella, but if he noticed the awkward silence building between them, he didn't comment on it.

When Wilson turned to leave, Isabella followed him without a word to Alec. All she wanted to do at the moment was crawl into bed and pull the covers over her head. She might need Alec's help to clear her name of murder, but she didn't have to admit how much his letters had touched her heart.

CHAPTER 9

Alec sat in a chair slightly apart from the other relatives as they gathered in the front parlor. Someone had turned on the electric window candles and plugged in the Christmas tree lights, infusing the otherwise somber gathering with holiday cheer.

Detectives Talbot and Mullins had arrived a few minutes ago and taken chairs behind the family members. Isabella chose a seat across the room from Alec. Having his confession interrupted made things awkward. Did she feel as uncomfortable as he did? Through his Army training, Alec had developed a good eye for reading people, but Isabella didn't give away much. If it wasn't for the faint blush on her cheeks, he'd have thought their conversation hadn't affected her at all.

But he cared very much what she thought because he had fallen under her spell through her letters. Spending time with her face-to-face only solidified those feelings.

"Thank you for coming today." Wilson glanced around the room, then sat down in the straight-backed chair in front of the fireplace, a sheaf of papers in his hand. He cleared his throat. "This is the last will and testament of Heloise Stratman Thatcher, dated October 30th of this year."

A collective gasp rippled through the group. By their reactions, it was hard to tell who had known Heloise had changed her will only a few months ago. Alec glanced around the room to gauge their expressions, which ranged from shock to unconcern.

"I'll dispense with the usual legalese, but I will read the statement Heloise included before the bequests." Wilson perched a pair of reading glasses on his nose. "'Family is important to me, as all of you have heard me mention over the years. Sadly, most of you haven't made family a priority. In fact, if I hadn't threatened to leave you out of my will, nearly all of you wouldn't have bothered to visit me. So, while we cannot choose our relatives, I choose to honor those who placed a priority on family. Besides my great-nephew Alec, not one of you regularly picked up a pen to write me or call just to check on a lonely, old woman.'"

Wilson paused to take a sip of coffee from a mug by his chair. "'One of you has been misrepresenting yourself to me, claiming a familial relationship that doesn't exist. To learn of this deception grieved me, and I changed my will accordingly. That some of you will be hurt by these changes is of no concern to me. I am too old and ornery to bother with worrying about your feelings any longer when, for all these years, you hardly had any care about mine.'"

Alec took a measured look around at how the relatives responded to these words of warning. Most kept their eyes averted, as if contemplating how much their inattention to Heloise might have cost them in this new will.

"'Because of that, I have decided to reward not based solely on blood,'" Wilson continued, "'but on genuine affection and care. To all who feel this is a cruel twist of fate, I offer no apologies.'" Wilson slipped the page into the packet of papers.

Alec let out a slow breath, as the tension in the room ratcheted up a notch. Titus scowled and crossed his arms across his chest, while Natalie narrowed her eyes, her hands clenching on her lap. Wilson hadn't given him the letter to read, only the will, so Alec focused on the most interesting part of Heloise's words: That someone in the room had "misrepresented" himself or herself. Had that "fake" relative killed her?

"How dare she say such things!" Charlton lobbed the first grenade, his cultured voice sharper than Alec had ever heard. The older man's face mottled with rage. "I came faithfully for decades to the old bat's insipid birthday celebrations, forced to endure desultory conversation and uninspired food. She better not have cut me out of her will because I didn't cater to her whims throughout the year." He shuddered. "Once a year was more than enough."

"You weren't the only one coming to see her to ensure we'd be remembered financially," Lorna snarled. "I'm counting on my share of her estate."

"To give to your son?" Janet narrowed her eyes. "We all know you've been bailing him out of his gambling debts for years, Lorna. Maybe now he'll have to face the music on his own."

"Don't act like you weren't borrowing against your own expectations." Titus turned to look at the others. "Janet's little business isn't doing so hot, but I heard she was able to secure a loan to keep it afloat based on her expected share of Heloise's estate."

Alec leaned back as if to avoid the bullets of words as the cousins shouted and raged against Heloise and each other.

"Stop it! Just stop it!" Isabella shouted as she rose from her chair. She stood trembling, her hands clenched at her sides, as the room fell silent. "Look at yourselves, attacking each other like wild animals. You only cared about Miss Heloise's money. She knew that was the only reason most of you came to see her once a year, but every year, she hoped it would be different. Each year, she told me that maybe this would be the year when someone would realize how lonely she was."

"That just made it easier for you, though, didn't it?" Titus also gained his feet, his finger jabbing toward Isabella. "You certainly paid attention to her, didn't you? You wormed your way into her good graces, then she changed her will." He swung around to Wilson. "What did Heloise leave the housekeeper?"

Alec stood, ready to defend Isabella from physical or verbal abuse.

"If you'll all be seated, I'll read the bequests." Wilson waited until Alec, Titus, and Isabella sat back down. Then he replaced his glasses and consulted the papers. "To Alec Stratman, my great-nephew, I leave half of my estate, including half of this house. May you use your inheritance wisely and fill the house with happy memories."

Alec kept his face impassive. Since he'd already read the will, only Heloise's letter had been a surprise. He scanned the room without moving his head to gauge the reactions of the others.

"To Isabella Montoya," Wilson said, "my faithful housekeeper of many years who has become more than like a granddaughter to me, I leave half of my estate, including half of this house. May you find your heart's desire in this arrangement." He put down the papers.

"That's it? Nothing for us?" Titus voiced the question surely the others were thinking.

"Heloise also left a few bequests to charities," Wilson replied.

Isabella's face leached of color. "I don't understand." Her eyes locked on Alec's. She rose unsteadily. "Miss Heloise shouldn't have done this. I can't accept it."

The confusion in her eyes propelled him out of his chair and toward her as the cousins began to argue again. He reached her side just as she started to crumple to the floor, his arms catching her and holding her close.

CHAPTER 10

❄

Isabella fought the desire to snuggle into Alec's strong arms as he held her close. With shouting continuing all around them, she couldn't fully relax.

"It's okay, I've got you." Alec spoke softly in her ear as he guided her from the room. "Let's go someplace quieter."

Grateful for his support, she stumbled alongside him down the hallway, her mind taxed with bits of information she struggled to sort. Alec's confession that he was the author of Jay's letters. The shock of learning how Miss Heloise divided her estate. The anger of the relatives at being cut out of the will. The wonderful, safe feel of Alec's arms around her. Once in the deserted kitchen, Alec helped her into a chair, then filled a glass with water.

"How are you?" He placed the glass in front of her.

She took a long sip before answering. "Better now, thanks."

Alec settled into the chair beside her. "For a minute, I thought you were going to faint. I was just as surprised that Aunt Heloise left her estate to us." A roguish grin crossed his face. "To be honest, if you had fainted, I would have been honored to come to your rescue.

The light-hearted statement startled a laugh out of her. "I see someone's been reading too many romance novels."

"I must admit that the circumstances would have been more frightening than romantic."

"The events of the last few days have been overwhelming." She took another sip of water, noting how her hand shook slightly when she replaced the glass on the table.

"Last night's arrest, spending the night in jail. Then the bail hearing this morning, your confession, the will—and the relatives shouting at each other. It's all . . ." Tears welled in her eyes. "Why did she have to leave me half of the estate? Now everyone will believe that I killed her, that I knew about the change. I would never hurt Miss Heloise."

Alec produced a handkerchief and gently wiped the tears off her cheeks. "I know you didn't hurt Heloise."

Isabella slumped in her seat. "You're the only one who does."

"I'm not going to rest until we find who's responsible." Alec scooted his chair closer to her and draped his arm across her shoulders.

"Me, either." She gave into temptation and leaned her head against his shoulder. For several minutes, neither one of them moved. She closed her eyes and let the warmth of his presence sooth her nerves. When the muscles in her neck began to throb from the slightly awkward angle, she reluctantly straightened.

Alec leaned back but didn't remove his arm. "We need to find who killed Heloise and Dean. The deaths have to be related."

"I agree, but how are we going to do that?" She finished the remaining water in one long swallow.

"Last night at dinner, I managed to ask who had access to the house the Sunday Heloise died, and only four relatives admitted to being here: Charlton, Titus, Lorna, and Janet. Digitalis can work fairly quickly, especially when ingested in food or drink, so one of them must have killed her. Does Keener know how Heloise got the poison in her system?"

"Not that I'm aware of, but wait a minute." She tapped her finger on the table. "I found Miss Heloise dead Monday. I usually have Sundays off to spend with my family. But Monday morning, I noticed the tea things hadn't been put away properly in the kitchen."

"Is that unusual?"

"Sort of." She turned toward him to explain. "Heloise often had a cup of tea in the afternoon, and on Sundays, she made it herself. I would wash and put the dishes away on Monday. But someone cleaned up the teapot, cup, and saucer because I found them in the wrong cabinet. I don't know why I'm just remembering this now."

Alec cleared his throat. "That must be how the poison got into her system."

"One of those four people must have made her tea and added foxglove leaves." Isabella fought back a fresh wave of grief. "Poor Miss Heloise."

He squeezed her shoulders before removing his arm. "I think we should tell Keener what we believe happened."

"That's a good idea." She pulled out her phone. "Oh, wait. He told me he'd be in court this afternoon, so I'll send him a quick text now." She sent the text and placed her phone on the table. "Do you think we should tell the detectives too?"

"Let's wait to hear back from Keener first. Maybe we can solve it ourselves since we have a pretty good idea how Heloise was poisoned and who could have done it."

"Okay." She tamped down the niggle of doubt that maybe this would be best left to the professionals. This was her life on the line. Surely with Alec on her side, they could solve the mystery, and she would be safe from prison.

"Isabella, how well do you know Charlton?"

"He only came by once a year like the others, but he's the closest blood relative because he's her first cousin. He often bragged about that when talking to the others after Miss Heloise went off to bed."

"What do you mean?"

She bit her lip, trying to recall exactly how Charlton put it. "He was very proud of the fact that he was the son of Miss Heloise's Uncle Thomas."

"And the others—how close where they to Heloise?"

"Mostly first cousins, once removed or third cousins, twice removed." At his blank look, she explained. "Heloise told me what that meant. Once removed is one generation farther away. Twice removed is two generations. So that means first cousins, once removed, are closer on the family tree to Heloise than third cousins, twice removed. Heloise came from a large extended family, so that's why it gets so confusing. Earlier this year, she hired a genealogist to plot out the family tree. She planned to surprise everyone on her birthday."

Alec frowned. "I don't recall hearing about that."

"That's because she hadn't talked to the others about it. I asked when we were planning the party, but she said she wasn't ready to unveil it yet. That's the last we talked about it." Isabella rubbed her forehead in an attempt to stave off a headache.

"Are you okay?" At her nod, he shifted so that he faced her. "So she knew that someone wasn't who they said they were. Remember what Heloise said in her will? She mentioned one of the cousins had claimed a familial tie that wasn't there."

"Oh, right." She thumped the tabletop. "Maybe that's why Dean was killed." More pieces clicked together in her mind. "At her birthday party this year, I overheard Janet talking to Titus about Dean's new hobby—genealogy—and how Dean had joked about ferreting out the family's secrets. None of them knew about Heloise hiring the genealogist, and she wasn't in the room at the time. Maybe Dean found out on his own who Heloise was talking about."

"That could explain why Dean was killed." Alec didn't sound as excited as she was. "But it still doesn't tell us who killed him."

"If we can figure out who Heloise meant, that would help, right? She left all her genealogical records in the study."

"Isabella..."

The tenderness in his voice touched a place in her heart she thought long dead after Jay's betrayal. She focused on the empty glass sitting on the counter, not trusting herself to meet his gaze.

"We need to talk about the letters."

"I know." She gathered her courage and looked at his face. "Do you think Heloise knew?"

Alec didn't ask what she meant. "I think so. She must have figured it out from your reading Ja—my—letters to her. She told me you did that sometimes."

Heat warmed her cheeks again. Heloise had teased her about Jay, then gently prodded Isabella to share his letters. The two of them had spent many an hour sitting together with a cup of tea as Isabella read the latest letter aloud. "After I read snippets from the first couple of letters, she started to ask me all the time if I'd gotten another letter—said it made her feel young again to hear the romantic words."

"That sounds like Heloise. In her letters to me, she always shared a tidbit about you, letting me know how special you were." He gently tucked a strand of hair behind her ear. "I think she was pitching me hints she knew I wrote the letters, but I missed the ball." He held out his hand to her. "But her legacy to us can wait. Right now, we have a pair of murders to solve."

She placed her hand in his without hesitation. He pulled her to her feet, the movement rocking her body into his. The contact against his muscular frame nearly made her gasp. She'd never experienced such an electrifying connection. Alec exuded danger of an entirely different sort.

❄

Isabella released his hand, then stepped back. Alec wanted to recapture it, but allowed her space to move away from him as he followed her to the study. Once inside the dimly-lit room, he surveyed the scattered papers on the desk, along with more spilled on the floor.

"I don't recall the room being this messy earlier." Isabella picked up a stack of papers from the floor. "Did the police do this?"

"No." Alec flipped the overhead switch to shed more light into the room. "There were papers on the desk when I found Dean. I checked the room again after the police released it, and it was basically the same."

She turned to face Alec. "Do you think someone was looking for the genealogical records?"

"Probably." He surveyed the chaos. Something niggled at the back of his mind, but he couldn't quite grasp it.

"I don't think they found what they were looking for." Isabella gathered up more papers, creating a thick stack in her hands.

He followed her lead and stooped to shuffle papers together. "If we assume that, where do you think those records could be?"

She set a thick sheaf of papers on the desk, then moved to another area to continue the cleanup, flipping through the documents as she worked. "That's a good question. Heloise kept important papers in her desk. If she didn't include the genealogy stuff with them, I'm not sure where she'd put them."

"Did she say or do anything out of the ordinary recently?" Not for the first time, Alec wished he had visited Heloise immediately upon his discharge from the Army six months ago, rather than cowardly staying away to avoid facing Isabella. If he had, he might have been able to prevent Heloise's death.

"No, only…" She stood with her back to the window that faced the side of the house.

"Only what?" He moved closer to her.

"I saw her kneeling by the fireplace in her room just a few days before she died. Heloise never messed with the hearth—said her knees were too old to be dipping up and down. She always let me do it. When I came into her room with her tea that day, she was on the ground by the hearth. I hadn't lit the fire yet—she liked a good blaze in the afternoon this time of year. I asked her what she was doing. She said something about dropping an earring."

"Maybe we should take a look at her room."

"The police went over it with a fine-tooth comb."

"*Ah*, but they might not have thought information about her family history significant." Again, that feeling he should be remembering something related to genealogy. "Who among the relatives do you think really cares about this family?"

She set down another stack of papers. "Dean liked the history part, but Natalie or Charlton had more pride in their connection to the

Stratman-Thatchers. You don't think one of them killed Heloise, do you?"

"I don't know." Alec pulled open the study door. "I just don't see the relatives caring so much about family that they'd resort to murder."

"People can get obsessed about their history." Isabella took one last look at the chaos. "Let's go."

As Alec relocked the study door, a shadow moved down the hallway. Jerking his head, he just missed whoever had been in the vicinity of the study. Unease followed him as he mounted the stairs after Isabella. He was beginning to think whoever killed Heloise wasn't the same person who killed Dean, which meant there were two murderers with two separate motives.

Outside Heloise's room, Isabella paused. "I haven't been in here since I found her."

He put his hand on her shoulder. She covered his with her own for a brief moment, then drawing in a deep breath, she opened the door.

Books covered the floor. The mattress had been tipped on its side with sheets and pillows shoved off the bed. The small curio corner cabinet had been knocked over, its figurines mostly in pieces on the floor.

"Who would do such a thing?" Isabella stepped into the room, Alec at her heels. "And when could this have happened without anyone knowing until now?" With a trembling finger, she pointed to the broken china. "She loved her collection of Dresden French court figurines, and now they're in a million pieces."

He firmed his lips, anger surging through his body at the vindictiveness of the room's devastation. "We should call the police."

"That won't be necessary."

Alec's reflexes shouted danger. He stepped in front of Isabella as he whirled around at the sound of a man's voice in the doorway. Charlton glared at them with a snub-nosed revolver in his outstretched hand.

CHAPTER 11

❄

*A*lec had pegged Charlton as the most concerned about his family connections, but he hadn't thought him capable of murder. The older man's steady hand on the gun made Alec revise that opinion.

"You two, move slowly over to the fireplace." Charlton kept the barrel aimed at its target. "Don't try anything—I'm a very good shot."

Alec positioned himself more fully in front of Isabella. He placed his hand on Isabella's arm to draw her along with him. With his body in front of hers, he took a step sideways in the direction of the fireplace. Another step and they stood in front of the grate.

"Good." Charlton came further into the room, his gun pointed at Alec's chest. "You can come in now, dear."

Lorna appeared in the doorway.

Isabella gasped. She inched closer to Alec, murmuring something under her breath that he couldn't make out.

"Alec." Lorna smiled. "You're not surprised to see me, too, dear cousin?" She closed the door behind her.

"Should I be?" He refused to let on that he hadn't considered her a suspect.

Lorna tossed him a saucy grin, then turned her attention to Charlton. "Did they find it?"

"I don't think so," Charlton said. "But I'm not sure it matters, now that this little trollop weaseled her way into Heloise's good graces and stole my inheritance."

"Our inheritance, you mean." Lorna folded her arms. "But she can't profit if she's convicted of killing poor Heloise, so her half of the estate will come to us."

"Not necessarily." Isabella spoke from behind Alec.

Charlton huffed. "What matters is that Heloise changed her will."

Isabella inched up beside Alec. "Did you kill her because she was going to expose you as the fake you are?"

"You don't understand." Charlton lowered the gun a fraction. "This family is everything to me."

Lorna rolled her eyes. "Really, Charlton, why must you get sentimental now?"

"Shut up, Lorna!" Charlton's voice cracked like a bullet.

The idea germinating in the back of Alec's mind since hearing Heloise's statement read aloud came into focus. "You're the fake. That's what Heloise meant when she said someone had been misrepresenting himself. She was talking about you, Charlton."

Lorna frowned. "We all knew Charlton's mother must have had an affair while your father was fighting overseas. That can't be the reason why Heloise was cutting you out of her will—she might have been old-fashioned, but she wasn't cruel."

Charlton swiped beads of perspiration from his brow.

"But that's not the reason, is it?" Isabella pressed. "It's because you're not Charlton Woods."

"Of course I'm Charlton Woods." He straightened, indignation lending steel to his voice. "Heloise has known me for years."

"DNA." Alec didn't realize he'd said the acronym aloud until everyone looked at him. "Earlier this year, Heloise had written to me about submitting a sample of her DNA to one of those genealogy companies, and she said something about sending the DNA from all the relatives to have a fuller picture of our heritage."

"She had no right to take our DNA without our permission!" Charlton realigned the gun to point to Isabella. "That nosy old woman must have collected samples when we were here last Christmas."

Isabella glared at Charlton. "The DNA showed you aren't related."

"I'm confused." Lorna turned to Charlton. "What are they saying?"

"That I've pulled the wool over everyone's eyes for many, many years," Charlton replied evenly.

"So you killed Heloise to stop the truth from coming out and to protect your inheritance." Alec wished Isabella had stayed closer to him, so he could protect her better. But she had edged even farther away. "And Dean must have found out about it."

"No, I didn't kill Heloise." Charlton's expression hardened. "But Dean shouldn't have taunted me with the truth. He'd worked it out on his own. Dean was always researching our family history, and he somehow discovered the truth."

"You killed Dean?" Lorna's eyes widened. She stumbled backward into the closed door.

Alec inched forward as Charlton shifted his attention to Lorna.

"I had to, my dear. He was going to tell everyone that I was an imposter." Charlton swept his eyes back toward Alec and Isabella before turning toward Lorna, who began to cry.

Alec propelled forward and swung his left leg to kick Charlton's right hand. The gun fell to the floor and Isabella dove for the weapon.

Alec grasped the older man by his right arm and twisted hard enough to force Charlton to his knees. Once he'd secured his grip on Charlton, Alec glanced at Isabella, who stood with the gun clutched in her trembling hands.

※

THE POLICE GATHERED EVERYONE TOGETHER IN THE FRONT PARLOR FOR another round of questioning after the incident with Charlton. Isabella had already given her statement and been asked to stay with the others. Being wrapped in a warm blanket next to a roaring fire didn't stop her shaking. Fearing she might spill the mug of hot tea one of the police officers had handed her, she put it on the end table. If Alec were here, she would be calmer.

"Alec still talking with the police?" Titus sank down onto the loveseat beside her, his bulk nearly dumping her onto the floor.

"I suppose so." She didn't want to sit so close to Titus, but lacked the energy to move.

"I can't believe Charlton killed Dean. Was it because Dean had found out that Charlton was a fake?" Titus shook his head. "But if he didn't confess to killing Heloise, then I guess you're still on the hook for that one, eh?"

Isabella used the blanket to create a wedge between herself and Titus. "I didn't kill Miss Heloise."

He held up a conciliatory hand. "I wasn't the one who was arrested for that murder."

Anger at his cavalier attitude flooded her body, steadying her nerves a bit. "I didn't kill her."

"Between you and me…" Titus leaned toward her, close enough that she caught a whiff of Irish coffee on his breath. "Is it true that Lorna and Charlton were an item?"

"Neither one said that." *Hurry up and rescue me, Alec!*

"Come on! You were there in the room."

"Why are you asking me all these questions?" Isabella reached for her tea, but one sip of the lukewarm beverage made her put it down again.

"Curiosity." Titus shrugged. "At this point, there's nothing else to do but speculate. I hope the police will finally let us leave."

Before she could comment, the door opened. Alec entered, along with the two detectives. Alec raised his eyebrows when he spotted Titus beside her. She bit back a smile at his obvious displeasure at the space next to her being taken.

"If I may have your attention?" Detective Mullins raised her voice to be heard over the murmurings in the room. "We arrested the man calling himself Charlton Woods, who has confessed to murdering Dean Sledge, and have taken Lorna Hermes in for questioning."

"Does that mean we can go home?" Janet called from across the room.

"Yes, you are all free to leave after you give us statements about today's incident." Detective Mullins gestured toward the group. "We will call you one at a time, starting with Titus Simons."

Titus heaved himself up, nearly tossing Isabella off the loveseat again, then followed the detectives from the room. Alec quickly crossed the room to snag the open seat beside her.

"I'm glad he was first—I was thinking up devious ways to dislodge him." Alec grinned at her. "How are you doing?"

"Better." *Now that you're here.* She dropped her voice to a whisper. "But if everyone leaves, how will we figure out who killed Heloise?"

"Come with me. I have an idea." He stood and held out his hand.

She unwrapped herself from the blanket and took his hand. "Where are we going?"

He tugged her along behind him, saying over his shoulder, "You'll see." She relished holding his hand as he led her up the stairs to Heloise's room. He paused in front of the closed door. "I think I know where Heloise put the family tree and DNA results."

Ducking under the police tape, he pushed open the door and led her to the fireplace. "When I was a teenager, she let me explore the entire house except for her room. One day, when I knew she would be out for several hours, I decided to poke around." He let go of her hand and dropped to his knees beside the hearth. "I was going to mention it earlier today, but we were *interrupted*."

Her heart beat faster as she examined the brick fireplace with her fingertips. Alec touched the bricks right below the mantle top. "Ah, here it is." He pressed his fingers into a crevice and suddenly, a portion of the side of the mantle popped open, revealing a small rectangle safe. Two slim envelopes rested in the space. He plucked them out and handed one to Isabella. "You open one, and I'll open the other."

She hesitated. "Shouldn't these be handed over to the police or Mr. Wilson?"

"Sure, after we open them." Alec had his already ripped open and was sliding out a folded paper. "Besides, we each own half of the house and its contents. Technically, these are ours."

"That makes sense." But she still felt strange opening an envelope Miss Heloise had sealed and hidden. Her envelope contained a single piece of paper. At first, she couldn't comprehend what the information meant, but then understanding dawned. At last, a stronger motive for someone else to kill Miss Heloise. Before she could share with Alec, he tapped his paper.

"It's the family tree, with notes in Heloise's handwriting in the margins. Here, look." Alec handed her the poster-sized paper and pointed to one entry on the far left.

Mildred Woods married Thomas Woods, son Charlton born 1943, died ?.

Heloise had written: *DNA results don't lie. Charlton isn't Charlton. Haven't found death date for real Charlton, but suspect it's sometime in 1960 when he was in South Africa.*

She looked at Alec. "So we were right. Heloise had discovered that Charlton was a fake."

"Charlton fooled us all, until Heloise submitted those DNA samples. I wonder how she got them."

"From paper cups." She rocked back on her heels. "She wanted me to serve the evening's hot beverages in insulated paper cups at last year's birthday celebration. She even had everyone write their name on the outside of the cup with a Sharpie. You know how eccentric Heloise could be—everyone went along with it without a quibble."

Isabella paused. "Family blood ties mattered more to Heloise than almost anything, so I'm not surprised she wanted to know everyone's DNA. But I'm not family. Why did she leave half her estate to me?"

CHAPTER 12

A scent of sweat wafted into the room, distracting Isabella. She jerked her head up and around to see Titus leaning against the doorjamb, his smile sending a shiver down her spine.

"That's a question we're all asking." Titus took a step into the room, his gaze on Isabella. "Now, give me those papers, and I'll be on my way."

Beside her, Alec tensed, then reached out his hand to clasp hers as he got to his feet, drawing Isabella with him.

She stood beside Alec, one hand clutching the documents, the other still nestled in Alec's grip. "No. I'm giving this to the police."

"I don't think you will." Titus cocked his head.

"You should leave now." Alec let go of her hand to move toward the other man.

"Not without the papers." Titus narrowed his eyes. "Isabella?"

"No." She inched farther away, her back connecting with the mantle. "Miss Heloise found out about how much money you lost in your Ponzi schemes." She raised the papers. "You conned several of her friends into investing in the last one."

"Give me the documents—or I'll tell the police what I overheard." Titus advanced farther into the room, fire in his eyes.

Alec blocked the man from coming any closer to Isabella.

"I have no idea what you're talking about!" She didn't care that her voice rose. "But if you don't leave this instant, I will scream the house down."

Titus focused on Alec. "She was engaged to your superior officer, but broke it off when she learned that you would inherit half of the estate from Heloise."

"What?" Isabella gaped at Titus, before glancing at Alec. With his body slightly in front of her, she couldn't see his expression.

Alec still faced Titus. "Is that so?" His voice dropped to an almost silky menace that made Isabella thankful she wasn't the one to whom the question was addressed.

Titus shot them a triumphant look. "When I came back after her birthday, I overheard Heloise talking on the phone. Heloise said Isabella had broken off the engagement after Heloise had hinted that Alec would be a co-inheritor along with Isabella. If I share that tidbit with the police, Isabella will have an even bigger motive for killing Heloise, don't you think?"

"It would if that indeed was what was said." Detective Talbot moved into the room. Relief flooded through Isabella at the sight of the detective.

"However," Detective Talbot continued, "one of our officers spoke with her next-door neighbor, Mrs. Hickory, this morning. She'd just returned from visiting her daughter in Florida, but stopped by the station as soon as she'd heard about Ms. Montoya's arrest. Mrs. Hickory was adamant that Ms. Montoya had nothing to do with Ms. Thatcher's death."

Titus snorted. "And you believe an old woman?"

Alec realigned himself with Isabella, his arm slipping around her waist. At least Titus's nasty allegation hadn't made Alec want to bolt.

"We believe the evidence," Detective Mullins replied as she joined her colleague in the room. "Mrs. Hickory put us in touch with a private detective hired by Ms. Thatcher. That PI had investigated all of the relatives, and discovered you had been rather creative with your finances, Mr. Simons. The private investigator turned over evidence of your illegal financial transactions."

"Those transactions are none of your business." Titus crossed his arms.

"The investigator said he has a paper trail showing how you conned the elderly into investing in companies that only exist on paper." Talbot eyed Titus with a grim smile. "And we have ample evidence Ms. Thatcher knew about those documents, which gives you a very strong motive to kill her."

"It still doesn't mean I had anything to do with Heloise's death," Titus spluttered. "That's hearsay."

"Since this isn't a court of law, it doesn't really matter," Mullins said. "We've subpoenaed your bank records, which I'm sure will shed more light on the subject. Meanwhile, the private investigator put us in touch with a moneylender, who told us that you've been steadily borrowing against your inheritance from Ms. Thatcher lately. You even told more than one creditor that you would be able to make good on your loans by the end of the year."

Titus thinned his lips.

"That's not all," Talbot continued. "We also discovered that you had been in the house the day of Ms. Thatcher's death."

"I admitted to coming back." Titus sounded more confident than he had when questioned about his finances.

"Mrs. Hickory gave our officers security video footage of you in the flower garden, snipping foxglove, the day before her death." Mullins nodded to someone behind her. "That's more than enough to arrest you for the murder of Ms. Thatcher."

"How do I know the video wasn't doctored with? It's entrapment!" Titus continued to bluster even as a uniform officer stepped into the room, read him his rights, and snapped cuffs on him.

Once Titus had been escorted, still protesting, from the room, Mullins turned to Isabella. "Ms. Montoya, the district attorney will be dropping all charges against you immediately."

Isabella sagged into Alec, who tightened his hold. "Is it really over?"

"Yes, it is." Alec dropped a kiss into her hair.

Isabella handed the papers from the envelopes to the detective, then laid her cheek against Alec's chest.

"Thank you." Talbot turned to exit after Mullins, but paused in the doorway to glance back to Isabella and Alec. "This isn't strictly relevant to the case, but Mrs. Hickory also told us that Ms. Thatcher was going to arrange it so that 'those two young people will finally realize how much they care about one another.' I wonder who Ms. Thatcher had in mind?" With a wink, he followed his partner out of the room.

Alec chuckled, and Isabella raised her head. "What's so funny?"

"I was wondering what plan Heloise had devised to bring us together." Alec gazed down at her.

She smiled too. "I'm sure it would have involved a royal flush—she seemed to like holding all the cards and revealing her hand in her own time."

"That's a pretty good description of Heloise." Alec tugged her closer.

She laid her head on his chest and closed her eyes, allowing the solid comfort of his arms to permeate her entire being. Heloise would be pleased if she could see them now. As she snuggled into Alec's embrace, Christmas now marked a new beginning for both of them.

EPILOGUE

❄

Tuesday, December 26

The dark blue suit that Alec wore reflected his somber thoughts. He smoothed his tie as he mentally prepared for the burial ceremony. Today, they would lay Heloise to rest in the family plot at Twin Oaks Memorial Cemetery. As per Heloise's wishes, none of the other relatives would be present. Just Alec, Isabella, and the Reverend and Mrs. Brown from the church Heloise had attended all her life.

Alec had hardly had time to talk to Isabella after the police arrested Titus three days ago. She had invited him to join her and her family on Christmas Eve and Christmas Day, but he'd declined. He needed time to think and hadn't wanted to intrude on the Montoya family's celebrations.

Now he couldn't wait to see Isabella again. He hurried down the stairs and stopped on the landing at the sight of her in a navy dress and hat, waiting by the front door. She looked up at him, a faint smile on her lips.

Alec walked down the stairs, a sadness that his aunt would miss seeing the two of them together settled on his shoulders. But Heloise would have been glad that she had brought them together at last. "Given the circumstances, you look lovely."

"Thank you." Her tone quivered a bit, and she brushed a stray tear from her cheek. "It's good to see you."

He took her hand. "How was your Christmas?"

"I always enjoy spending time with my family." She paused, "But I missed you."

"Isabella, I've been thinking." He had done nothing but think for two straight days.

"Yes?" Her eyes sparkled.

A man could stare into those dark eyes and never get tired of the sight.

"It might not be the appropriate time or place, but I don't think Heloise would have minded." This was harder than he thought it would be. He should have written her instead. He was good with words on paper.

"Go on." Isabella smoothed down his lapel.

"What do you think about turning this house into a bed-and-breakfast?" Alec hadn't meant to lead with that, but his insides were so jumbled, he hadn't been able to get out the important thing first.

"A B&B? That's a great idea." Isabella glanced around the foyer. "Miss Heloise would have loved sharing this house with others."

Drawing in a deep breath, he plunged on. "That's not all I wanted to talk to you about."

"It's not?" She met his gaze.

The hopeful note he detected in her voice gave him courage to continue. "I love you. I fell in love with you through those letters. Meeting you in person only confirmed that I want to spend the rest of my life with you."

A smile grew across her face, and this time it reached her eyes.

Dropping down to one knee, he took her left hand in his. "Isabella Montoya, will you do me the great honor of marrying me?"

She remained motionless for what seemed like an eternity, then all of a sudden she tugged at his lapels, silently urging him to his feet. She wrapped her arms around his neck. "Yes, I will marry you."

She pulled back. "I love you, Alec Stratman."

Alec cupped her face in his hands. Emotion caught in his throat but he swallowed hard. "And I love you, Isabella Montoya."

He'd kept his promise to Heloise. From this day forward, he would spend the rest of his life cherishing the gift of Isabella's love.

The End

A SNEAK PEEK AT PROTECTING HIS WITNESS

❄

U.S. Marshal Chalissa Manning settled into a steady pace as she ran the gravel loop ringing Burke Lake. She noted the mile marker as she swerved around a mom power-walking while pushing a jogging stroller. Whitney Houston belted "I Wanna Dance With Somebody" into her earbuds, the pulsating beat from the 1980s hit in rhythm with her stride. Saturday morning sunlight streamed through the trees lining the pathway. Another mile marker flashed by. Good, she was on pace to finish a 5K run in nineteen minutes.

She enjoyed running, loved being wrapped in her own world while the miles zipped by. So far, her transfer from the St. Louis, Missouri, office to Arlington, Virginia, had gone smoothly. After four years in St. Louis, she'd been ready for a different city and more challenging opportunities in her career with the U.S. Marshal's Witness Protection Service. For her, the career clock ticked a little louder, given she had become a Marshal shortly before her thirtieth birthday, while most of her colleagues had entered the service directly after college graduation. Her previous work with troubled youth in residential treatment centers had made her a good fit for witness protection, but being older than most of the other newbies meant she had more to prove—and less time to do it if she wanted to make the Marshals her career. Which she did.

"Help!" a male voice shouted as Chalissa came up on the marina parking lot. "My son's missing!"

Without hesitation, she veered off the path and into the parking lot, stopping her music and pulling her earbuds out. Several groups of people stood in small clusters near the fishing pier. A tall man wearing jeans and a long-sleeved flannel shirt topped by a vest with multiple pockets approached one of the clusters, his voice raised enough for Chalissa to hear.

"Have you seen my son?" The group shook their heads collectively, and the man moved onto another group, asking the same question and receiving the same reply.

Chalissa jogged up to him and touched his arm as the man turned away from the group. "Sir? Maybe I can help you."

The man whipped around so fast he nearly bumped into her. "My son's gone. He was here just a few minutes ago," his voice cracked. He swallowed hard, then continued, "I've got to find him."

"Okay, we'll find him. Tell me your name." Chalissa pitched her voice low and soothing to project calm in the midst of this man's personal storm.

"Titus. Titus Davis." Mr. Davis started to walk away, but Chalissa plucked at his sleeve to bring him to a halt.

"Mr. Davis, my name is Chalissa Manning." She waited until she had his attention once more. "I'm with the U.S. Marshal Service."

She pointed to indicate her cropped leggings and baggy T-shirt. "I'm obviously not here on official Marshal business, but let me help you find your son."

"You're with the Marshals?" Mr. Davis's shoulders relaxed a little at her nod. "Thank goodness."

"Have you called the police?"

"No." He shot a hand through his hair, sending the brown strands every-which-way but didn't volunteer any more information.

"How long would you estimate your son's been missing?" Chalissa took her phone out of its arm band and opened the notes app.

"Five minutes." Mr. Davis had returned his gaze to scanning the area.

"Mr. Davis." Chalissa waited until the man looked at her. He had a very attractive face, with its strong jawline and short-cropped beard. Chalissa mentally shook her head. The man had a son, which meant he either had a wife or a significant other. "I know you want to look for your son, but these questions will help us find him."

"I'm really worried." Mr. Davis swiped at his eyes. "He's only seven and on the spectrum."

"He has autism?" She blurted out her question before thinking, as memories slammed into her.

"Yes, it's not severe, but it does impact the way Sam interacts with people," Mr. Davis said. "He doesn't read social cues well, and can be too trusting."

"In what way?" A vision of Brandon engaging cashiers, dog walkers, and anyone else who came to his attention zipped across her mind.

"If someone asked Sam to help him look for a lost puppy, he'd do it in a flash." He rubbed his chin. "Even though we've discussed the dangers of going off with a stranger over and over again. Listen, I really need to go look for him."

Chalissa shook her head as if the movement could clear her mind from thoughts of Brandon, but the pain was just as sharp as it had been sixteen years ago. But Brandon wasn't here, and Sam needed her help. "Please bear with me. The more info I can gather, the quicker we can involve more people in looking for your son."

Her words succeeded in stopping him from walking away, but he balanced lightly on the balls of his feet, ready to leave in an instant. Better get on with her questions. "What was Sam wearing?"

"He had on jeans, sneakers, a long-sleeved blue T-shirt, and a bright orange fishing vest."

She jotted down the description. "Hair, eye color, height?"

"His hair is a little lighter brown than mine," Mr. Davis gestured to his head. "His eyes are brown and he wears glasses. They're bright green, the kind that wrap all the way around the back of his head.

And he's about yea big." He held out his hand to indicate close to three feet.

"Thank you, that's very helpful. Where did you last see him?"

"It was down by the pier." He pointed to the fishing pier. "We had set up to fish—see the blue camping chairs about midway down on the left side?"

"I see them." She noted the location, then added the information to her notes.

"Sam realized he'd dropped his favorite lure. He'd been holding it along with his pole as we walked from the car to the pier." Mr. Davis drew in a breath. "We're parked right there." He nodded toward a late model, dark blue crossover SUV in a parking space a few feet away. "I didn't see the need to walk with him."

Chalissa visually measured the distance from the chairs to the SUV—about fifty feet.

"He's nearly eight, and we've been working on him doing things by himself because…"

"A boy needs his independence," she finished the thought for him.

"Yeah," he agreed.

"But you watched him all the way to the car?"

"Yes. I saw him pick up the lure—it was on the ground right by the back passenger-side door, where he must have dropped it as he got out of the car."

Mr. Davis closed his eyes briefly, pain etched into the lines of his face. "Then I got a text. I only looked away for a few seconds."

"From your wife?" As soon as the words left her mouth, Chalissa wanted them back. At least her voice had sounded brisk, professional, and not inquiring.

"No." Mr. Davis looked away. "My wife, Sam's mom, died when he was a baby."

She winced for pouring more pain on an already-painful situation. "I'm so sorry."

"Thank you." He squared his shoulders. "I read the text, and when I looked up again, Sam wasn't there."

"You didn't answer the text?"

"It was spam." His gaze locked with hers. "You don't think it was sent on purpose to distract me from Sam? Let me show you." He pulled out his phone and brought up the text. As she read the short message, he continued, "It was something about my credit card account, but my credit card company doesn't communicate that sort of information by text."

"Thanks." The text had standard spam language, but given the timing, she noted the sender's number just in case. "Where have you looked for your son?"

"All around here."

"Excuse me?" An older man wearing the brown uniform of a park employee approached them. "Are you the father with the missing boy?"

"Yes, I'm Titus Davis."

"Nathan Wiltshire." He turned toward Chalissa. "And you are?"

"Chalissa Manning, U.S. Marshal." She shook his hand. "I left my official ID in my vehicle, but while running on the trail, I heard Mr. Davis calling for help." She held up her phone. "I've taken down all the pertinent information about what happened, including a description of Sam, age seven. If you'll give me your contact info, I'll send it to you to disperse to the park employees."

Mr. Wiltshire rattled off his phone number. "That will make things easier."

"I have to look for Sam," Mr. Davis said. "I can't just stand around doing nothing."

The park employee shook his head. "It's best if you stay here, in case Sam comes back on his own." He held up a hand as Mr. Davis opened his mouth. "I know how difficult a request that is. If it were my son, I'd want to be searching the grounds too. But it really is best if you leave the search to park workers and the police."

"You've called the police?" Chalissa asked.

"Yes, as soon as I heard the boy was missing." A shadow passed over Mr. Wiltshire's face. "Another Northern Virginia park had a similar incident about five years ago and the Northern Virginia Park Authority management made the decision that any time a child was reported missing on park grounds, the police would be brought in immediately."

Chalissa heard the sorrow behind the words and hoped Mr. Davis hadn't picked up on the inflection. That incident probably hadn't turned out well, but there was no need for Mr. Davis to start imagining anything darker than he already was.

The other man extended his hand to Mr. Davis, who shook it impatiently. "Hang tight. I'll keep you updated. I'm going to make sure everyone is looking for your son."

As the park employee walked away, Chalissa turned back to the father. "Is there anyone I can call for you?"

"Call?" His eyes widened. "No, I'll take care of it. Excuse me."

She watched him move toward his vehicle, fear and concern slumping his shoulders. The knot in the pit of her stomach tightened even more. She could relate to how terrified Mr. Davis must be feeling, how helpless, particularly since his missing son had special needs. For a moment, the temptation to cry out to God to save Sam, to not let Brandon's fate befall him, overwhelmed her. But personal experience had confirmed God didn't answer her prayers.

❄

Hanging onto his control by a wire as thin as the fishing line on his rod, Titus leaned his back against the rear bumper of his SUV. Tremors shook his hands and it took him three tries to select the right number to call.

"Mac here."

U.S. Marshal James "Mac" MacIntire's familiar, crisp greeting nearly made Titus cry out in relief. "It's Titus. Sam is missing."

"What happened?"

Titus quickly recounted the events of the morning. "The park has started a search and called in the local police."

"Could Sam be playing a game?" Mac's question irritated Titus.

His son knew better than to play a game like this, but he bit his tongue to prevent himself from taking out his fear on Mac. "I don't think so. Sam usually follows the rules."

"Did you and Sam run into anyone you know at the park?"

"No." Titus could hear the fear in his own voice. "With the trial coming up in a couple of weeks…" He let the thought trail off, knowing Mac would understand.

"You did the right thing in calling me."

"Mr. Davis?"

Titus raised his head and met the direct gaze of Chalissa Manning, a serious expression stamped on her face. "Hold a minute, Mac." He put the phone down.

"The police have arrived." She pointed over her shoulder to where a trio of officers made their way through the crowd toward him. "I'll brief them while you finish your call."

"Thanks." Titus put the phone back to his ear as she moved toward the officers. "The police are here."

"Good. Who was that you were talking to just now?"

"Chalissa Manning. A jogger on the path who heard me shouting for Sam. She offered to help. She said she was a U.S. Marshal, but she didn't have any identification on her." The tranquility and compassion in her eyes as she questioned him had done much to calm him during those first few moments of panic at the realization Sam was missing.

"You didn't say anything?" Mac's question stung.

"Of course not," Titus snapped. "I merely gave her the information necessary to find Sam." He lowered his voice, his gaze seeking out Chalissa, where she stood talking to the police. "I certainly didn't blurt out I'm in witness protection."

"Good. We do have a new inspector who arrived last week from the St. Louis office, but I haven't met him or her yet." Mac cleared his throat. "Unfortunately, I'm four hours away in southwestern Virginia, but let me check with the office on the new inspector. If it is this Chalissa Manning, I'll call and brief her, so she can take over as your point-of-contact during the search."

"Okay."

"For now, follow protocol and don't say a word to anyone about your being in WITSEC."

"Got it." Titus ended the call as Chalissa waved him over. As he walked toward the group of officers, the same prayer looped over and over in his mind. *Please God, keep Sam safe. Don't let him be hurt because of me.*

To find out how this ends, purchase *Protecting His Witness* on Amazon for print and Kindle, or at your favorite e-reader retailer!

A NOTE FROM THE AUTHOR

Thank you for reading *Mistletoe & Murder*. I hope you enjoyed getting to know Isabella and Alec! If you enjoyed this book, please leave a review on Amazon. It does help others find my work.

ABOUT SARAH HAMAKER

Sarah Hamaker has been spinning stories since she was a child. While she's had two traditionally published nonfiction books, her heart is writing romantic suspense. You can find a list of her books, listen to her podcast, "The Romantic Side of Suspense," and connect with Sarah on her website, sarahhamakerfiction.com, or on these social media platforms:

Amazon Author Page: https://www.amazon.com/-/e/B002TIARBS

BookBub: https://www.bookbub.com/profile/sarah-hamaker

Facebook: https://www.facebook.com/authorsarahhamaker

Goodreads: https://www.goodreads.com/author/show/1804799.Sarah_Hamaker

Instagram: **sarah.s.hamaker**

LinkedIn: https://www.linkedin.com/in/sarah-hamaker-7295a01/

Pinterest: https://www.pinterest.com/hamaker0041/sarah-hamaker-fiction/

OTHER BOOKS BY SARAH HAMAKER

Dangerous Christmas Memories (Love Inspired Suspense)

A witness in jeopardy…and a killer on the loose.

Hiding in witness protection is the only option for Priscilla Anderson after witnessing a murder. Then Lucas Langsdale shows up claiming to be her husband right when a hit man finds her. With partial amnesia, she has no memory of her marriage or the killer's identity. Yet she will have to put her faith in Luc if they both want to live to see another day.

Illusion of Love (Seshva Press)

A suspicious online romance reconnects an agoraphobe and an old friend.

Psychiatrist Jared Quinby's investigation for the FBI leads him to his childhood friend, Mary Divers. Agoraphobic Mary has found love with online beau David. When David reveals his intention of becoming a missionary, Mary takes a leap of faith and accepts David's marriage proposal.

When Jared's case intersects with Mary's online relationship, she refuses to believe anything's amiss with David. When tragedy strikes, Mary pushes Jared away.

Will Jared convince Mary of the truth—and of his love for her—before it's too late?

Protecting Her Witness (Seshva Press)

A family in danger…a U.S. Marshal sworn to protect.

U.S. Marshal Chalissa Manning has been running from her past and God for most of her life. When she meets widower Titus Davis and his son, Sam, her well-built defenses begin to crumble. But someone is targeting Titus and Sam, and it's up to Chalissa to both protect them and to find out who is behind the attacks.

As the threats pile up, will Chalissa be able to keep the family she's grown to love safe?

Coming in July 2022…

Vanished Without a Trace (Love Inspired Suspense)

Made in the USA
Middletown, DE
06 December 2024